"Stop manha **led.**

"Oh, baby, wha︙ ⎯laughed. "Now I get to make the o⎯ous comeback—that you've been begging for a man to handle you."

"And you accused me of talking in clichés—besides, it's completely untrue."

"Honey, when a woman runs from a man the way you just did, it's the equivalent of an engraved invitation for him to go after her and catch her."

She forced herself to meet his gaze. "Or it could mean she can't stand to be around him, that she's had enough of his pigheaded, stubborn—"

Caleb pushed her against the wall and pinned her there, between it and his body. The fire in his eyes was hot enough to burn, and she felt its molten effects deep within her. Bracing one hand near her head, he leaned into her, his body heavy and hard against hers. "Admit it. This is what you planned to have happen when you ran out here."

His head lowered to hers until his mouth was a tantalizing inch above her lips. She ached for the feel of his mouth on hers. She'd been aching for it ever since he'd kissed her the night before, been wanting more, wanting him again. But she didn't want to give him the satisfaction of knowing it. "I will not succumb to your caveman tactics!"

He smiled, then brushed his lips lightly, seductively, across hers, wooing her instead, and her defenses crumbled. . . .

WHAT ARE *LOVESWEPT* ROMANCES?

They are stories of true romance and touching emotion. We believe those two very important ingredients are constants in our highly sensual and very believable stories in the *LOVESWEPT* line. Our goal is to give you, the reader, stories of consistently high quality that may sometimes make you laugh, sometimes make you cry, but are always fresh and creative and contain many delightful surprises within their pages.

Most romance fans read an enormous number of books. Those they truly love, they keep. Others may be traded with friends and soon forgotten. We hope that each *LOVESWEPT* romance will be a treasure—a "keeper." We will always try to publish

LOVE STORIES YOU'LL NEVER FORGET
BY AUTHORS YOU'LL ALWAYS REMEMBER

The Editors

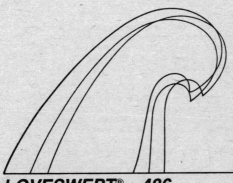

LOVESWEPT® • 486

Barbara Boswell
Strong Temptation

BANTAM BOOKS
NEW YORK • TORONTO • LONDON • SYDNEY • AUCKLAND

STRONG TEMPTATION

A Bantam Book / August 1991

*If you would be interested in receiving protective vinyl
covers for your Loveswept books, please write to this address
for information:*

> *Loveswept*
> *Bantam Books*
> *P.O. Box 985*
> *Hicksville, NY 11802*

ISBN 0-553-44151-5

Published simultaneously in the United States and Canada

*Bantam Books are published by Bantam Books, a division
of Bantam Doubleday Dell Publishing Group, Inc. Its trademark, consisting of the words "Bantam Books" and the
portrayal of a rooster, is Registered in U.S. Patent and
Trademark Office and in other countries. Marca Registrada.
Bantam Books, 666 Fifth Avenue, New York, New York
10103.*

PRINTED IN THE UNITED STATES OF AMERICA

OPM   0 9 8 7 6 5 4 3 2 1

One

"*After she passed through the orphanedge harshly, then she was a teacher for a little girl who lived with a man named Mr. Rochester and his crazy wife locked up in the attic, but wasn't really their child. The house burned down and the crazy woman died. Mr. Rochester was blind but happily, he married Jane.*"

Cheyenne put down the paper and rubbed her temples with the tips of her fingers. She adjusted the desk lamp and glanced around her bedroom, as if searching for an escape route. There was none, of course. This was her life, another school term teaching another class of sophomore English students.

She stared in dismay at the papers stacked on the desk. What was truly daunting was that Heather Lane, author of this mangled critique, was one of the better students in her first period English class. Even worse, Heather's paper was the best of the ten she had read so far; the sentences were complete and had some semblance of punctuation.

Cheyenne thought of the previous essay she'd read, which had sported one solitary period for the entire paper. Another had so many misspellings, the words had been almost indecipherable. At least Heather's *orphanedge* was somewhat phonetic.

It was obvious the Whitneyville sophomore class needed extensive guidance to hone their writing skills, and it was up to their teacher, Cheyenne Whitney Merrit, to provide it.

"Cheyenne?" A dark-eyed teenager with a tangle of red curls swept up in a thick ponytail, stood beside the open bedroom door, peering tentatively inside.

"Come in, Joni Lynn," Cheyenne said, smiling at the girl.

"I hope I'm not interrupting." Joni Lynn entered the room, clutching a typewritten paper in her hand. "I wondered if you would look over my"—she paused and gulped—"college essay."

"I'd be delighted." Cheyenne took the paper and began to read. Her lips curved into a proud smile. Like everything Joni Lynn wrote, this essay was as close to perfection as any English teacher or college admissions board could ever wish for. Her ideas were original and fluently expressed, her choice of words superb, her grammar impeccable. Reading the essay was a genuine pleasure.

"It's wonderful, Joni Lynn," Cheyenne said, turning her smile on the girl. A teacher was blessed with a uniquely gifted student like Joni Lynn Strong perhaps once in a lifetime, if she were lucky. As this September marked the beginning of her fourth year teaching English at Whitneyville High School, Cheyenne considered herself truly privileged to have encountered Joni Lynn so early in her career.

She had recognized the girl's talent instantly, from the first writing assignment she'd given Joni Lynn's sophomore English class two years ago. Joni Lynn's efforts had glimmered like a jewel in the slush pile of grammatical horror.

Cheyenne flushed with embarrassment as she remembered how she had checked the last name on the top of Joni Lynn's paper at least three times to make sure she'd read it correctly. *Strong.* Joni Lynn was a *Strong*? Cheyenne had been shocked at that stunning revelation. One did not expect outstanding writing talent from the Strongs. In fact, nobody in Whitneyville expected anything from the Strongs but trouble.

Having grown up in Whitneyville, Georgia, Cheyenne was well versed in Strong lore. She'd heard them called everything from "poor white trash" to "spawns of Satan." It was rumored that the first Strongs in the town were Yankees, whose arrival was somehow linked with General William Tecumseh Sherman's scourged earth policy. They had been deliberately sent, the story held, to add insult to Whitneyville's war-inflicted injuries. A less combative historical view had the original Strongs driven by a blood feud from some primitive Appalachian mountain lair.

Whatever their origins, the Strong clan still lived on the wrong side of the tracks, literally, down by the river in a cluster of dilapidated frame houses that shook when the trains thundered by. Not that Cheyenne or any other "nice girl from a good family" had ever ventured down there for a closer look. They all had been raised on the dangers of "what the Strongs might do" and took the threat seriously.

The legends persisted, fed by exaggerated stories of the latest Strong escapades. Cheyenne often silently credited the tellers of those with a fine grasp of the art of fiction, and didn't think much more about the Strongs. Other good citizens of Whitneyville still warned their offspring against the degenerate Strongs, whose numbers continued to grow. The previous year, when Cheyenne had invited Joni Lynn to live in her house as a sort of baby-sitter/mother's helper/errand girl, everybody had been aghast.

"You're going to take in a *Strong*?" Tricia Vance Harper, Cheyenne's friend since their kindergarten days, had asked incredulously. The way she pronounced the name left no doubt that she found it analogous to toxic waste.

"Let a *Strong* into your house," warned Willie, the owner of Whitneyville Groceries, "and before long, the place will be crawlin' with 'em. You'll never get rid of 'em." He spoke of roaches in much the same way.

"*A Strong?* Living here, on our block?" howled the Mayfields, Cheyenne's across-the-street neighbors. "The property values of the whole neighborhood will plummet."

But Cheyenne had always had a stubborn streak. Having seen Joni Lynn's potential, having gotten to know the girl well during her sophomore year, she would not be diverted from her goal. Which was threefold: To rescue Joni Lynn from the Strongs, to provide her with the nuturing atmosphere the gifted child deserved, and to see her get into a top-rated university where her talent could be polished and fully utilized.

Joni Lynn desperately wanted to make something of herself and her life, and Cheyenne was determined that she would succeed.

So last September, one year ago, town history was made when a Strong moved into 100 Silver Creek Road, the oldest, most distinguished street in Whitneyville. Contrary to dire predictions, property values in the neighborhood remained stable, and no other Strong but Joni Lynn was ever seen in the area. Life in Cheyenne's household continued peacefully. The neighbors even grew accustomed to the sight of Joni Lynn walking Peppy, the family dog, and taking little Brittany and Jeffrey Merrit to the Whitneyville Newsstand for Popsicles.

"You're the only one in town who could've pulled it off, Cheyenne," Tricia often said with a grudging admiration. "Being a Whitney gives you the license to do things that would result in instant social death for anybody else. Only a Whitney could take in a *Strong* and not be totally ostracized and reclassed as one of them. Your social position here is truly unassailable."

Cheyenne always demurred, but she knew her friend was probably right. Her maiden name commanded an awesome respect in the town. Though she now used the surname of her late husband, Evan Merrit, she was always acknowledged as a Whitney, a direct descendant of Edward Whitney, who had founded the town in the 1830s.

"Do you really think it's good enough, Cheyenne?"

Joni Lynn's anxious voice interrupted Cheyenne's reverie. She rose and gave the girl a swift hug. "It's much better than good enough, Joni Lynn. With your academic record and SAT scores, you'll be able to get into any school in the country."

Joni Lynn's face flushed with pleasure. "My family is so excited that I'm going to go to college," she said softly.

Her remark surprised Cheyenne. Joni Lynn never mentioned her family, although Cheyenne was aware that she visited them regularly.

"I want to make them all proud of me," Joni Lynn added earnestly, her huge dark eyes shining.

Privately, Cheyenne thought that making the Strongs proud shouldn't be all that difficult. Staying out of jail ought to do it. But she didn't voice her thoughts to Joni Lynn. She understood family loyalty.

At that moment, Peppy, their mixed collie-retriever-springer spaniel, bounded into the bedroom, his leash in his mouth. He looked from Cheyenne to Joni Lynn and whined hopefully.

They laughed at his eagerness.

"I'll take him out for his walk," Cheyenne said. "I need some fresh air to clear my head from the noxious effect of *those*!" She pointed to the offending stack of sophomore papers and made an exaggerated grimace.

"Poor *Jane Eyre* gets bashed again?" Joni Lynn guessed. "As if her life wasn't hard enough!"

Cheyenne fastened the dog's leash to his collar and let him lead her out of the room and down the wide center staircase. "I'll be back soon," she called to Joni Lynn.

It was a clear, warm September evening, and thousands of bright stars shone in the night sky. Peppy lived up to his name, straining energetically at the leash while trying to run along the sidewalk. He knew where they were going, to a vacant wooded lot two blocks away that was frequented by all the neighborhood dogs.

As she hurried along behind the dog, Cheyenne heard the vibrating sounds of a motorcycle's engine. A motorcycle on Silver Creek Road? she mused, perplexed. Impossible. She decided that the noise must be coming from Shiloh Drive, several blocks away. She'd heard that one of the Wilson boys had purchased a small Honda bike. Secluded Silver Creek Road was so quiet that faraway sounds frequently carried, especially at night.

The engine noises grew louder, and the roar forced her to conclude that the motorcycle was indeed on Silver Creek Road. She frowned. If that earsplitting clamor woke her Brittany and Jeffrey, whose bedrooms were in the front of the house facing the street, she would have a talk with Tommy Wilson at school tomorrow and assign him an essay on decibels and noise pollution.

The sound grew nearer, but paradoxically quieter. It took Cheyenne several moments to ascertain why. When she did, her heart lurched violently and began to thunder in her chest. The motorcycle had slowed down, its engine idling. It was close behind her, cruising slowly along the side of the street. Stalking her?

Peppy seemed oblivious to it all. He pranced along, his tail high in the air, clearly delighted to be outdoors. The motorcycle pulled alongside of them now, keeping pace with them. Cheyenne continued to walk, keeping her eyes straight ahead, looking neither to the right nor the left, pretending to be as oblivious to the machine's presence as Peppy was.

"Well, well, who have we here?" The voice was a masculine one, husky, low, and definitely mocking. "Miss Cheyenne Whitney, the town princess herself, out for a stroll."

Cheyenne's legs seemed to lock, and she came to an immediate halt. She stood stock-still, too unnerved to move or speak or even breathe. Peppy tugged against the leash, protesting their sudden stop.

"Enjoying the night air, Miss Cheyenne?" the deep male voice purred. The question was an unmistakable parody of the good manners practiced by the town gentry.

In spite of herself, Cheyenne turned her head to stare at—what? She couldn't call him an attacker. Not yet. Her knees began to tremble, and she swallowed hard.

Her gaze first flicked nervously over the black monster of a machine he was riding, an enormous Harley-Davidson that looked as if it could run right over Tommy Wilson's little Honda and leave no remains.

She saw one powerfully muscled thigh encased in black jeans, straddling the cycle, a scuffed boot resting on the pedal. Slowly, her gaze drifted upward, over the rider's flat belly and wide belt buckle to the expanse of muscular chest and broad shoulders. He wore a black T-shirt, and his bare arms were as hard and muscled as the rest of him.

She blinked rapidly when she spied the tattoo of a coiled cobra on his upper arm. Though it was partially hidden by the cuff of his shirt, she would know that tattoo anywhere.

"Caleb Strong!" she exclaimed, even before she looked at his face. He was the only person she'd ever known who had a tattoo, and a memorable one it was. The cobra on his arm had its own tattoo, an image of another smaller cobra imprinted on its body. Both cobras were baring their fangs in a deadly reptilian smile.

"You remember me?" Caleb asked, his rakish smile somehow as dangerous as the cobras on his arm. "I'm honored, Miss Whitney."

Eyes wide, she stared at his face. He looked older than the last time she had seen him. Of course, that had been fourteen years ago, when she'd been a fourteen-year-old freshman at Whitneyville High School and he'd been an eighteen-year-old senior. Few Strongs remained in school long enough to reach their senior year, but Caleb had. He had, however, negated that accomplishment by quitting school and leaving town several months before graduation. There had been rumors about . . .

She looked away from him. There were always rumors about the Strongs, which were never actually denied or verified, and a new one invariably sprung up to replace the ones that had faded.

She cleared her throat. "It's Cheyenne Merrit now." She wished that her voice hadn't wavered.

"Oh, yeah, I heard you got married. Merrit, huh?" He sounded amused by her choice. "A local boy. Very fitting that a Whitney should marry a Merrit. Keep those aristocratic Southern bloodlines pure."

"He's dead," she said defensively. She kept her gaze firmly fixed on the pavement as she admonished herself for blurting it out in such a bald manner. What had happened to her characteristic aplomb?

"My deepest sympathy to the grieving widow," Caleb said politely enough, but she picked up the subtle, ironic edge in his tone. It was as if he knew. . . .

No, that was impossible, she assured herself. Nobody knew, not even her closest friends. And most especially not Caleb Strong, who had left town years and years ago.

"I didn't know you were back in Whitneyville," she said nervously, veering from the subject of Evan

Merrit, their marriage, and his untimely death. She focused her eyes on Peppy who had flopped down on the sidewalk with a long-suffering whimper.

Caleb shrugged. "Well, here I am."

"Yes, I see." She groped for some polite bit of chitchat. "Are you married?" Her cheeks flushed, and she caught herself shifting uneasily from one foot to the other. It was a perfectly natural question to ask, she thought. So why was she blushing? And why couldn't she stop this ridiculous fidgeting? She'd never fidgeted before in her life!

"No, I'm not married." A derisive smile curved his sensual mouth. "The holy state of matrimony has always seemed downright unholy to me. Sort of like prison, but worse. At least the state pen gives you time off for good behavior."

"Yes." She forced a thin social smile, while wondering at his prison reference. Had he been an inmate himself? "Well, welcome back to Whitneyville."

It occurred to her that this was the longest conversation she'd ever had with Caleb Strong. Her encounters with him that single year they'd both been at Whitneyville High had been extremely brief.

But definitely memorable. She gulped, remembering.

"I get back to visit the family every year or so." He flashed a crocodile smile. "Of course, my arrivals and departures are never mentioned in the *Whitneyville Gazette.*"

She thought of the weekly *Whitneyville Gazette*'s Comings And Goings column in which Whitneyville residents' vacations were detailed and the visits of former citizens or their relatives were duly recorded. No Strong had ever been mentioned in that column.

"As a matter of fact," he added, "I was in Whitneyville last summer for a brief visit. Shortly before you took my sister Crystal's girl to live with you."

Cheyenne tensed. Crystal Strong was Joni Lynn's mother, one year older than Caleb. She had left high school at sixteen to have her baby out of wedlock. Joni Lynn never mentioned her father, although she had made several negative comments about a stepfather.

"I met your sister at school several times last year," Cheyenne said cautiously. They had talked about Joni Lynn's talent and potential and the possibility of her moving in with Cheyenne.

In her mind's eye, Cheyenne pictured Crystal Strong. In spite of appearing chronically tired and dispirited, she still bore a remarkable resemblance to her pretty daughter. The woman had mentioned a divorce and three younger children, one of whom was in trouble with school authorities for habitual truancy. Crystal had been surprised, even a little suspicious at first, of Cheyenne's desire to help Joni Lynn, but had finally given her permission for the move.

"Have you come to see Joni Lynn?" Cheyenne asked, and a wave of anxiety surged through her. This was the first time any of the Strongs had come to visit, and she worried what it might portend. Surely he wouldn't attempt to take the girl back to the Strongs and a futureless future?

"I am allowed to visit my niece, aren't I? Or do I have to have a security clearance before setting foot on these hallowed grounds?"

His tone was light, teasing, but contained an underlying vein of cool sarcasm.

"Of course," she said. "That is, of course not!" Gracious, which question was she answering anyway? Once again she shifted uneasily, and once again her face flushed with embarrassment. Her students would never recognize this flustered young woman as the firm and unflappable Mrs. Merrit. No one in town would ever believe that the poised and perfect Cheyenne Whitney Merrit was capable of an unpolished moment.

"Now, what exactly do you mean, Mrs. Merrit?" Caleb drawled.

She cast a furtive sidelong glance at him. To her great discomfort, he was staring at her, his dark brows arched, his mouth curved into a smile that could only be described as mocking. And arrogant. Perhaps self-confident, if one wanted to give him the benefit of the doubt which nobody in Whitneyville ever gave to any Strong. Piratical was closer to the mark. And sexy. Very sexy.

Cheyenne's mouth was suddenly dry. Strongs might be antisocial, but they had been blessed with an overabundance of good looks and sex appeal, which only served to compound the town's aversion to them. Had the Strongs been physically unattractive, they wouldn't be so dangerous to the community's impressionable young, went the traditional argument. And following that conventional wisdom, Caleb Strong was most definitely a threat and always had been.

The glow from a nearby streetlight illuminated the hard-edge, handsome features of his face. His dark blond hair, cut shorter than in his high school days, was sun streaked, and his mouth was well shaped, the lower lip sensually, temptingly full. His deep tan made his blue eyes as vivid and clear as a summer sky. They seemed to glow, too, with a vibrant intensity and energy that beckoned and compelled and intrigued. . . .

Cheyenne felt a taut, almost painful thrill. She remembered looking into his blue eyes long ago, on a day in early October when she'd been on her way home from junior varsity cheerleading practice. She could still visualize the scene in her mind, see herself in the short blue-and-white skirt and oversize sweater of her uniform, her hair pulled to each side in pigtails and tied with blue and white ribbons.

She'd been taking a shortcut through an alley near the high school, hurrying to get home before the sun faded completely from the early evening sky. Caleb, riding a roaring black motorcycle—the very same one he was riding tonight?—had appeared seemingly from out of nowhere and screeched to a stop alongside her.

"If you can believe your eyes and ears," he'd said with a caustic drawl. "It's Little Miss Whitney, slumming on the poor side of town."

Cheyenne remembered that her heartbeat had quickened as she gaped at him, at his disreputably long hair, at his sulky, sensual mouth and the cigarette dangling between his lips. He'd been wearing jeans and a white T-shirt, and the cobra tattoo on his arm had seemed to sway when he flexed his muscle to shift the bike's gear.

She had mumbled some excuse about missing her ride and that she was in a hurry to get home before dark. Even as she spoke, she could imagine how he saw her, as a prim and proper goody-goody girl, one he would never plaster up against his locker in a steamy X-rated embrace, like the kind that had gotten him and Penny Sherwood suspended from school for three days.

Cheyenne had observed that notorious, torrid scene on her way to gym class several weeks earlier, and the sight had lingered in her mind for weeks, months afterward. She could even conjure up memories of it today! She had never seen anything so carnal, not even in the movies. Penny Sherwood had been clinging to Caleb, her arms wrapped around him and one of her legs draped over his hip while he rubbed his hands all over her body, his mouth clamped over hers. It had been profoundly shocking, yet it had aroused the strangest, most peculiar feelings within Cheyenne, feelings she didn't understand. She knew they were wicked yet they'd been too pleasurable to banish.

"You wanna ride?" the teenage Caleb had asked her casually, stunning her with his invitation. For a few paralyzing moments she'd been tempted—oh, how she'd been tempted—to climb astride that evil black motorcycle.

Of course, she hadn't done it. Tamping down her shocking renegade impulses, she had shaken her head and refused with a polite "no thank you."

After all, she was a good girl, a Whitney, who didn't dare risk her reputation by riding on the back of Caleb Strong's motorcycle, her arms wrapped around his waist as they zoomed through the streets of Whitneyville.

"Scared?" he had taunted.

She'd held her head high and said no, she simply preferred to walk.

He'd laughed knowingly and continued to follow her through the alley until she emerged onto the main street. "Next time, take the long way home and stay out of alleys," he had called as he gunned the engine. "Otherwise, you might run into some big bad wolf on a motorcycle who'll drag you out of your safe little world." Then he was gone, his laughter mixing with the roar of the bike.

And here they were again, fourteen years later. A strange giddiness swept through Cheyenne as she met his gaze, his eyes piercing and intense. She felt as if he were looking inside her, through the veneer of the ever sensible and reliable good girl who had never allowed anyone to drag her out of her safe little world.

"Are you going to invite me in to visit my niece?" His voice broke the peculiar spell that held her in thrall. "Or should I arrange to see her at Crystal's place? After all, there are your neighbors to consider. I'm sure the prospect of having a Strong on the block must've scared them witless. If more of us start appearing, they're liable to go completely mental."

His words, spoken lightly with such taunting insouciance, were so close to the truth that Cheyenne blushed. "You're very blunt," she said in a strangled tone.

"True. I leave the sugarcoated doublespeak to ladies like you, Miss Cheyenne."

She was so unnerved, she dropped the dog's leash. "Everybody thinks the world of Joni Lynn," she said, trying desperately to get the conversation back on a safe and neutral track.

He laughed. "Then they probably think she was switched at birth or something. That in some perfectly proper and respectable home, a faultless Whitneyville family is baffled and tormented by their changeling Strong offspring who has always been a misfit, from the day she was carried home from the hospital. Not being born a Strong would naturally explain Joni Lynn's totally unStronglike characteristics."

Cheyenne winced. Incredibly enough, two weeks ago Martha Mayfield had expounded on a similar theory. The Mayfields found that easier to fathom than the unimaginable likelihood of a *Strong* being talented and ambitious, moral and personable.

Peppy chose that moment to tug against the leash in an impatient attempt to get moving again. There was no resistance, since Cheyenne hadn't yet picked up her end. Peppy gave a triumphant bark and dashed off, taking full advantage of his unexpected freedom.

"Peppy, come back!" Cheyenne cried. She watched the dog hightail it down the block. "Peppy!" Her voice rose and turned into a command, a command that the exuberant dog failed to heed. Peppy raced away, never looking back.

"Peppy cuts loose," Caleb remarked.

"He's never been out alone at night before," Cheyenne said anxiously. "He escaped once during the day, and we didn't find him for hours. A neighbor finally called and said she'd seen him down on Route Six, dashing back and forth across the highway. He was almost hit three times!"

"Sounds like the Pepster's freedom went to his

head. The same thing happened to my cousin Bo right after he got out of jail the first time. He was so wild, he was back in the slammer twenty-four hours later."

"Oh." A feeling of unreality swept over Cheyenne. She'd never heard anybody toss off a casual remark about the jailing of a relative, but then she'd never known anybody who had a relative in jail.

Then she saw the gleam in Caleb's impossibly blue eyes. His remark had not been a throwaway one at all, she realized, but one intentionally calculated to shock her. As if he had deliberately chosen to say the type of thing a woman like her would expect to hear from a man like him.

She stared at him, astonished by the sudden insight.

"Maybe I'll go chase ol' Peppy down," he continued, a smirk crossing his face. "Catch him and take him home. Dog stew makes mighty fine eatin'. It's a delicacy for us Strongs."

She knew then that he was mocking her and the whole town for their unrelentingly poor opinion of the Strongs. "Oh, stop it!" she said sternly. "I don't believe for one moment that the Strongs eat dogs!"

"Ah, the lady is an enlightened citizen with liberal views. But tell me, madam, would you let your son or daughter *date* a Strong?"

"Since my daughter is six years old and my son is only five, I don't think the question is relevant."

"A nice, neat evasion, Miss Cheyenne. You're a well-mannered lady through and through. And certainly too well-bred and too careful to take the foolish risk of climbing on the back of my motorcycle to go look for your dog."

His wicked, confident smile taunted her, as if he knew she wouldn't dare accept the challenge blazing in his eyes.

A totally unexpected and confounding surge of wildness, of recklessness, burned through her. She was amazed that she could even identify the feelings since she'd never done a wild or reckless thing in her life.

As Caleb Strong well knew.

She drew in a deep, shaky breath. Her heart was thundering, and she felt oddly light-headed. He was so smugly certain that she would never take a single step out of her safe little world.

Well, what did he know? asked a previously unheard and defiant little voice in her head.

"I'll accept your kind invitation to search for Peppy," she said, and took a halting step toward the monster machine.

Two

Caleb laughed softly. "You surprise me, Miss Cheyenne." He gestured toward the bike's passenger pillion behind him. "Get on."

Cheyenne glanced down at the flowing skirt of her blue-flowered Laura Ashley cotton shift. She felt the first falterings of her resolve.

"Pull up your skirt and climb on," he urged in a seductive, beguiling whisper.

She shivered a little. Surely the snake had used a similar tone when urging Eve to take just one bite out of that nice shiny apple.

"Maybe I'd better not." She cleared her throat, but her voice sounded husky and thick anyway.

Caleb's hand snaked out and caught her wrist. "But you want to, don't you, Cheyenne?" he teased in that same lilting, mesmerizing cadence.

The way he said her name was compellingly intimate and, she noted dizzily, he had dropped the mocking, distancing "Miss."

She felt the strength of his fingers encircling her wrist. His action had brought them closer, close enough for her to feel the heat emanating from his body. So close, in fact, that if she moved forward just another few inches, she would be touching him.

"Are—Aren't you supposed to be wearing some sort of a helmet when you ride?" she asked in a high, reedy voice that bore no relation to her usual well-modulated tones. "I bought two of those child-size helmets for my children, Brittany and Jeffrey, and I always insist that they wear them when they're riding their bikes. Of course, neither of them have learned to ride without training wheels but they—"

"Do you always babble on like this when you're nervous?" Caleb asked, amusement glimmering in his eyes.

"I'm not babbling and I'm not nervous," she retorted quickly, her face scarlet with embarrassment.

"Oh, but you are. I shake you up, don't I, Cheyenne?"

How was she supposed to answer that? she wondered, cringing at her idiotic behavior. She was painfully aware that she was acting like an uptight Victorian spinster who always succumbed to the vapors when in the company of a virile young man. Her eyes were drawn compulsively to Caleb Strong. He was certainly virile. If she really were a Victorian spinster, she'd have already keeled over!

"I do admit that I—I'm not c-comfortable engaging in this type of conversation," she stammered. Even to herself she sounded stuffy and prim.

He laughed wickedly. "Take it one step further, honey. You're not comfortable in engaging in any type of conversation with a Strong."

"I converse very easily with Joni Lynn and she's a Strong."

"Except Joni Lynn, then."

Part of her wanted to make a quick excuse and run home to safety. She'd never participated in this type of confrontational banter before. She had dated Evan exclusively through four years at Whitneyville High, then four more at the University of Georgia before marrying him a week after their college graduation. Since his death four and a half years ago, she'd had only an occasional date and always with the type of solid gentleman who respected her position as a Whitney and as a widowed Merrit. That type of man did not *banter*, nor did he encourage a lady to pull up her skirt and hop onto the back of a motorcycle!

"If you don't make up your mind soon," Caleb said, "that dog of yours will be halfway to the state line."

He stroked his thumb slowly and deliberately over the inside of her wrist, and she felt warmth radiate through every nerve in her body. She wondered if he could feel her pulse beating triple time.

He could. Caleb Strong was well versed in women's sexual responses, and Miss Cheyenne was too inexperienced to mask hers. His mouth curved into an ironic smile. She was nervous and wary of him, but she was attracted to him too. His gaze slid lazily over her. How surprising. How damned amusing! Starchy Cheyenne Whitney getting turned on by the notorious ne'er-do-well, Caleb Strong.

What surprised him even more was that he felt an undeniable tug of attraction to her too. Aristocratic ladies-to-the-manor-born were definitely not his type. He and his family had been scorned, snubbed, and otherwise hurt by those icy paragons once too often. They ranked at the bottom of his list of sexual turn-ons.

But when he looked at Cheyenne, he saw an irresistible ash-blond woman with alabaster skin, classic high cheekbones, a perfect nose, and a sensual mouth with full pouty lips. His gaze lingered on those lips, and he felt a flash of heat in his groin. Hers was definitely not the thin-lipped, pursed mouth of a bloodless aristocrat. Lord, what he could do with a kissable mouth like hers! What she could do with it to him . . .

Their gazes collided once again, and he was astonished to see a cool-fire hunger burning in her big hazel eyes. It was at total variance with the demure, shapeless lines of her dress and the no-frills barrettes that clipped her shoulder-length hair back from her face.

He released her wrist, but she didn't move. Another surprise. At the very least, one would expect a Whitneyville lady to jump like a scalded cat away from the touch of a Strong. It occurred to him that he didn't really know Cheyenne Whitney Merrit at all, although he'd know *of* her forever, long before their paths had crossed in high school all those years ago.

Everybody in town knew the Whitney family. They served as Whitneyville's unofficial icons. Cheyenne Whitney had been one of the prettiest girls in Whitneyville High School, although he'd never lusted after her then or even considered asking her out. He had been a rebellious hell-raiser back then, but he hadn't been stupid. He'd known that no decent girl of her class and station would go near a boy like him. He had learned at a very early age what it meant to be a Strong in Whitneyville.

"I offered you a ride on my motorcycle once before," he said suddenly. "Years ago, way back in high school." He saw her eyes widened in surprise. "Of course, you wouldn't remember that."

"I remember. I didn't think you would."

"You said no. I wholly approved."

She stared at him, confused. "You—You did?"

"Sure. As a member of Whitneyville's First Family, you had high standards to uphold. I would've been shocked and disappointed if you hadn't lived up to them."

Cheyenne's teeth fastened nervously over her lower lip. She didn't know what to say. He was mocking her and the town again, and she had no quick, witty rejoinder to toss back at him.

Fortunately, he didn't seem to expect one. "So, do you want to look for your dog or not?" he asked, not bothering to conceal his impatience. Or his indifference.

He didn't care if she went with him or not! she

thought. For some reason that rankled. She was considering taking the first wild and totally out of character step in her life and he wasn't even interested. Perhaps that was what gave her the courage to gather her skirt to her knees and swing her left leg over the thick black leather seat.

She swiftly arranged the voluminous folds of her cotton skirt until only her bare calves were visible, swinging down alongside the bike. Still, he made no attempt to hid his blatant study of her legs.

Caleb liked what he saw. Her toenails were painted a surprising bright pink, and her feet looked sexy in flat-heeled strappy sandals. His gaze traveled up her legs, and he noted that her ankles were slender, her calves firm and shapely, her skin a creamy ivory. He couldn't help but speculate about her thighs, concealed beneath the yards of blue-flowered cotton. He imagined them, white and soft and rounded, opening to him, for him. . . .

The surge of rampant sexual heat that flooded his body shocked him, and he had long considered himself unshockable. He coughed. It was a fake cough, but at least it covered the groan he had involuntarily emitted.

It was definitely time for some action to divert him from his perverse thoughts. "Hold on," he ordered as he revved the engine.

The machine thrust forward. Cheyenne uttered a small squeak of terror and instinctively grabbed on to him. He accelerated, and they rocketed down the road.

Without even realizing it, she inched forward on the seat until she was pressed tightly against him. Her thighs hugged his hips, and she wrapped her arms around his waist, clinging to him. His muscled back was warm and hard, and she buried her face against it, squeezing her eyes shut.

She'd never been so frightened in her entire life. It felt like they were flying. It was exhilarating, it was terrifying. A rush of adrenaline pumped through her veins. She was completely unfamiliar with its effects—the heightened alertness, the speed-racing pace of her heart, the wild urge for physical action. Somehow, she felt sick and wonderful at the same time. She wanted to scream, although whether with laughter or tears, she wasn't sure.

Hers was not, and never had been, an adrenaline-producing life. If thrill seekers were rated on a scale from one to ten with ten being a race-car driver whose hobby was skydiving, then she was a minus one.

Caleb steered the motorcycle into the dark, wooded three-acre lot where she and Peppy originally had been headed. Since Silver Creek ran through the middle of the property, it had been designated as a flood plain and was therefore considered unbuildable, despite its location in the center of a highly desirable residential neighborhood.

"If I were a runaway dog, this would be my first stop," Caleb said, braking the bike to a halt. "Let's take a look around here for him."

The bike might have come to a stop, but Cheyenne didn't loosen her grip, or move from her position. She was plastered against him as close and tight as wallpaper on a wall.

He turned his head to look at her. "Are you okay?"

She was *not*. She was mute with terror and unable to unlock her rigid limbs.

"Ah, the thrill of the sensation of speed!" he rhapsodized. "Nothing like it." Unpeeling himself from her inexorable embrace, he climbed off the bike and stood beside it. Her eyes, he saw, were glassy with fear.

"I hate the sensation of speed," she said, "as much as I hate the sensation of hairpin turns on one wheel at ninety miles an hour." She shuddered "It's about as thrilling to me as a cardiac arrest."

"You probably don't have much fun at amusement

parks," he said dryly. He put his hands around her waist and lifted her off the bike.

Cheyenne found herself clutching his forearms for support. Her knees felt distinctly rubbery. "I feel like kissing the ground," she said, managing a weak smile. "Like the Pope does when he gets off an airplane."

"Maybe I went a little too fast for your first time," Caleb conceded. He didn't remove his hands from her waist. Instead, he widened the spread of his fingers until they spanned her body from the undersides of her breasts to the curve of her hips. "I probably took those turns too fast for a beginner too."

Their eyes met and held for a long moment. Cheyenne was the first to look away. Her gaze drifted down, focusing on his big hands holding her. It was an affecting sight. She had to remind herself to breathe.

"You'll like it better next time," he said. His long, strong fingers started to move, lightly caressing her.

She wondered how he managed to make those innocuous words sound so devastatingly sexy. Her mouth was dry, and she moistened her lips with the tip of her tongue.

A silence charged with sexual tension hung between them. Cheyenne stared at him; she couldn't seem to drag her eyes away. Since he'd been seated on his motorcycle earlier, she hadn't realized how tall he was. He stood at least a couple inches over six feet and seemed to tower over her own five feet four inches. She had to tilt her head to meet his eyes.

His superior height and strength made her feel petite and feminine and sexier than she'd ever felt in her life. The unfamiliar feelings he evoked confused her, and alarmed her. She was no dreamy-eyed schoolgirl who indulged in romantic fantasies. She never had been. She was Cheyenne Whitney Merrit, steel magnolia, relentlessly strong, practical, and logical. Yet she couldn't seem to take a single step away from him, or do anything to break his hold on her.

A slow, sexy smile curved his mouth. The knowing glint in his eye told her that he was fully aware of his effect on her, that he knew all about the yearning ache that kept growing inside her. A hot flush spread from her forehead to the tip of her toes, yet the restless longing welling up inside her was stronger than her embarrassment at him knowing she was aroused.

He lowered his head so that his mouth was only a few inches above hers. "Do you want me to?" he asked, his voice deeply masculine.

She quivered at the sound of that voice. And at the question. *Was he asking if she wanted him to kiss her?* He knew that she did! But he expected her to say so, to tell him? The thought made her mind spin. Did he want to humiliate her? Make her plead with him? Or was that the way things were done nowadays? She'd never been kissed by anyone but Evan, and their relationship had not been conducted in the brave new world of adult dating.

"I—I don't know how to answer that," she stammered at last, lowering her eyes from his.

He grinned. "It's not a trick question, honey."

"I don't know why you even asked it!" she cried, chagrined.

"You mean a gentleman doesn't always ask first? Hmm, I'll store that away for the next time I masquerade as one." He dropped his hands and stepped away from her. "Here, Fido," he called, raising his voice. He whistled. "Come on, boy."

One moment she had been close to him, on the verge of kissing him. The next she stood alone, trembling from the potency of the voluptuous feelings he had unleashed within her. Had he merely been toying with her? "The next time I masquerade as a gentleman," he'd said. *He had been making fun of her the entire time!* Humiliation washed over her in great waves.

"The dog's name is Peppy," she said tightly. Hot tears filled her eyes, and she quickly blinked them back. She needed only to cry in front of him to make her mortification truly complete.

She scurried away from him, heading deeper into the woods. As she called Peppy's name, her voice cracked.

A playful bark answered her, and Peppy charged boisterously toward them. "Peppy!" Cheyenne stooped down and held out her arms to him. "Come here, Peppy. Good boy!"

Peppy came closer, but just as she made a grab for the dangling leash, he bounded off. He was back a moment later, stopping just out of her reach.

"He thinks this is a game," Caleb said, coming to stand beside her.

Cheyenne said nothing. She started toward Peppy, calling his name in a coaxing tone. The dog let her come a few feet closer, but the moment she reached for the leash, he took off again, barking exuberantly.

"Peppy the psycho mutt." Caleb rolled his eyes. "He sure isn't a dog I would've picked out as yours. Seems like you'd have one of those pocket-size pedigreed breeds with the unpronounceable names. You know, the ones that get special haircuts and wear fancy ribbons."

"And cost hundreds of dollars," she said tersely. "We got Peppy at the county animal shelter for five dollars when he was just six weeks old, and we couldn't love him more."

"A practical rich girl, hmm? Commendable, Mrs. Merrit."

She had been called Mrs. Merrit every single day for the past seven years, and it had never before grated on her nerves. But hearing Caleb Strong say it in that sardonic drawl of his set her teeth on edge. As for his "rich girl" charge . . . She clenched her hands into tight fists. He couldn't have been further off the mark with that one.

Though the Whitney name remained golden, a series of poor investments by her grandfather and father had all but obliterated the once-formidable estate. She had inherited nothing but the Whitney house on Silver Creek Road, which had been built by her grandfather's grandfather. Evan had died uninsured, and the rest of the Merrits, upper middle class but not wealthy, did not help her financially. She needed her teaching job at Whitneyville High to support her family. Thousand-dollar pedigreed dogs were not an option in her life. There were times when even necessities were not options for her and the children.

She was not about to confide her financial status to Caleb Strong, though. He would probably delight in her reversal from "have" to "have-not." At the very least, he would make some jocularly stinging remark that she would remember for the rest of her life.

She turned her full attention to her dog again, chanting his name until he reappeared.

Peppy loved this game so much, he played it three more times, coming close enough to entice Cheyenne to make a lunge for him, then dashing off with a joyfully triumphant bark.

"This could go on all night," Caleb said with an impatient sigh.

Cheyenne made no response. She stood rigidly, her back ramrod straight as her eyes scanned the wooded darkness for the dog.

Caleb was undeterred by her silence. "Hey, I have an idea! Let's appeal to his Lassie instincts. I'll grab you like this." He caught her shoulders, whirled her around, and dragged her against him. "Now you struggle. Yeah, just like that. And call the dog. His protective instincts will be aroused, he'll come to save you and then we'll grab him."

"Let me go!" she cried, struggling fiercely.

"Ouch! Not so rough! Hey, that was uncalled for, Cheyenne! No kicking or scratching! You're overacting. You're only supposed to pretend to—"

"This isn't for the dog's benefit," she panted, still fighting him. He didn't loosen his grip on her. "It's for real. Let me go! I won't let you make a fool out of me again!"

With a deft, swift movement, he hauled her firmly against his solid body. One big hand captured both of hers and held them behind her back. He curved his other hand around the nape of her neck to hold her head in a viselike grip. Thrusting one powerful thigh between hers, he used his legs to completely immobilize her.

"Let me go!" she repeated, wriggling against him. With her limbs secured, all she could move was her torso, and she did so, furiously.

The feel of her soft body rubbing against him struck Caleb with another swift, fierce jolt of longing. Her continued squirming intensified it. "If you don't cut it out right now, I'll assume you want to take the consequences," he muttered between clenched teeth.

"Consequences of what?" she demanded, not ceasing her struggle for freedom.

This time Caleb was unable to mask his groan of arousal. "Of *this*!" He thrust his hips provocatively against her.

Feeling the unyielding fullness of his arousal, Cheyenne immediately stilled her movements, paralyzed by the intimacy.

They were both silent for a long, tension-charged moment. Then Caleb asked in a hoarse voice, "What did you mean, make a fool out of you again?"

"You know very well." Her tone wasn't as severe as she'd intended it to be. He had readjusted his hold on her, and now his hard arousal was pressing insistently against the softest, most vulnerable part of her. She was achingly aware of her breasts crushed against the hard wall of his chest. Her nipples felt tight and tingly, and she was aware of a shockingly wanton impulse to rub them against him.

"I don't play word games, lady. If I ask a question, it's because I don't know the answer."

She made a sharp exclamation of disbelief.

"What was that snotty *ha* for?" he asked.

"As if you don't know."

"I don't know!" His voice rose with frustration. "I don't even know what we're talking about. Or fighting about, for that matter. And we're going to stay here like this until you tell me."

"You deliberately humiliated me!" she exclaimed, and was astonished by her outburst. Once again he'd driven her out of her shell of polished poise. Once again she'd blurted out exactly what she had been thinking, rather than a cool and unrevealing perfunctory response.

"I did what? When?" He stared at her.

He couldn't be that obtuse! Cheyenne decided he was taunting her again, and rage burned through her. "You asked me if I wanted you to." She flung his own words back at him, then instantly wanted to recall them. If she had wanted to further humiliate herself, she couldn't have done a better job, she thought grimly.

"I did, didn't I?"

He was so cool, while her composure was practically nil. She felt another flare of anger at the perverse injustice of it all. "Yes, you did. Because you're cruel and calculating and deliberately set out to humiliate me." There, she'd said it, for better or worse. "Now let me go."

He didn't. "You thought I'd set you up to humiliate you," he repeated. "You're way off base with that one, lady. I don't get my kicks that way."

"Don't call me *lady* in that—that insolent tone." She gave a small ladylike sniff, then narrowed her eyes and said icily, "And if you don't let me go immediately, I'll . . ."

"You'll what?" Caleb's angry confusion drained away, and his eyes, his smile, became devastatingly seductive. "Call for your faithful dog to come to your rescue? Sorry, baby, I don't think that'll work. It's obvious that Peppy has never seen a Lassie flick and has no idea that he's supposed to come charging in to save you. Now can we talk about what's really bugging you?"

"What's really *bugging* me"—she emphasized the word scornfully, because it was one that she, a self-respecting English teacher, would never normally use—"is that you're imprisoning me in a Neanderthal grip, when all I want is to get my dog and go home."

"That's all you want, huh?"

"Yes."

"And the reason you went ballistic is because I'm imprisoning you, not because I didn't kiss you when you wanted me to."

She stiffened, then began her struggling anew.

"Whoa, hold on a minute, you little wildcat." He made a sound that was somewhere between a husky chuckle and a deep groan. "I didn't deliberately plan to humiliate you. Hell, you must've known that I wanted you—as much as you apparently wanted me."

She didn't like the sound of that. "I don't want you!"

"Everybody in this town would certainly believe that," he said sardonically. "But if I were to try to tell anyone in Whitneyville that the exalted Cheyenne Whitney wanted me, a *Strong*, to kiss her in a dark wooded lot, do you think a single person would believe me? Hell, not even my own family would!"

She stared up at him. "What are you saying?"

"That I wanted you to be damn sure you knew what you were doing before you did anything with me. Because if you suddenly felt violated by touching me and started screaming, guess who'd be arrested for assault?"

He released her wrists and dropped his other hand

from her neck. To his surprise, she didn't instantly scuttle away from him. She didn't even seem to realize she was free. If she did, she wasn't doing anything about it. She remained standing in front of him, so close that their bodies were still touching. When he looked down into those serious, liquid eyes of hers, his senses began to swim.

"Arrested?" she repeated breathlessly. Her hands dangled uselessly at her sides. Hesitantly, hardly allowing herself to think about what she was doing, she raised them to rest lightly on his chest.

Instantly, his arms went around her again, though he held her loosely this time. She could feel the pressure of his linked hands at the small of her back. Sensual heat stirred within her. It was difficult to focus on anything but the wild, fierce sensations his nearness so effortlessly evoked within her, but she forced herself to listen to him.

"Yeah, arrested," he was saying. "And I don't relish getting beaten to a bloody pulp while in my jail cell, which is what happens to town lowlifes who forget their station and get too close to Whitneyville ladies."

Though the night air was warm and humid, Cheyenne felt a chill run through her. "That's pure Southern gothic fiction," she protested. "Things like that don't happen here."

"Not to anyone in your circle. But it does happen to others, even now, in the nineties. My kid cousin Rusty didn't believe it either, until six months ago when it happened to him."

"What happened to him?"

"Lily Thurman happened to him. She was home from college on spring break and started flirting with Rusty. He was working at Wheaton's Gas Station back then, and they started seeing each other on the sly."

Cheyenne remembered Lily Thurman as a student at Whitneyville High, bright, pretty, a cheerleader, a member of the top social clique. She struggled to place Rusty Strong, but had no recollection of him. The Strongs who weren't troublemakers were invisible to the community.

"Poor Rusty." Caleb shook his head. "He fell hard for Lily and managed to forget the First Commandment of Whitneyville: 'Know Your Place and Keep It, Especially if You're a Strong.' What happened is the archetypal *Town Without Pity* scenario. One night Rusty and Lily were parked in that grove down by the river when a group of her friends, also home from college, drove in with a couple cases of beer. The grove hasn't changed any since we were kids. It's still the place for underage drinking and sex."

Cheyenne gulped. She'd never gone near the notorious grove, had never indulged in drinking or sex when she was underage. It occurred to her that she didn't indulge in them now either, though she was well past the legal age.

"What did Lily and Rusty do when the others arrived?" she asked, well aware that it would not bode well for Lily Thurman's reputation if she were discovered with a Strong.

"What's a nice girl like Lily to do when caught in a compromising position with a Strong?" Caleb asked. His voice hardened, and his blue eyes were as cold as a Nordic winter. "Why, scream for help, of course. Claim to be abducted and assaulted."

"Oh, no!" Cheyenne gasped. "She didn't!"

"Rusty was arrested and put in jail," Caleb said grimly. "He spent his nineteenth birthday there. Nobody was allowed to see him for three days, then he was taken directly to the hospital. The official report read that he had sustained injuries while resisting arrest. It was a damn lie. He'd been worked over in his cell, at Lily's father's request. My aunt Peggy, his mother, called me in hysterics."

"That's terrible!" Cheyenne said softly. She was horrified by the brutality, the blatant injustice. *A Town Without Pity*, indeed.

She tried to remember something, anything, she'd heard about Rusty Strong's arrest six months ago, but had no recollection of any of it. Of course, the various Strongs' periodic trips to jail were not considered newsworthy, or even interesting gossip, so the tale might not have circulated.

But an incident involving Lily Thurman, the attorney's daughter whose family had lived in Whitneyville for generations, was an entirely different matter. Surely, she would have heard something about that. But no one, not even Joni Lynn, had mentioned a thing.

"The whole case," Caleb said as if reading her mind, "including the arrest, was hushed up, and so was Rusty's hospitalization. The charges against him were eventually dropped."

She wondered how all of that had been accomplished.

"After all," he added bitterly, "we wouldn't want sweet little Lily's name dragged through the mud, now would we?"

"But what about Rusty? He was arrested on false charges, he was jailed and beaten and hurt! Couldn't *he* file charges or sue or something?"

"Yeah, sure, baby. Maybe when pigs fly." Caleb laughed harshly. "Rusty is a Strong, remember? Strongs are second-class citizens in this town. You know it as well as I do."

What he said was true, of course. Cheyenne couldn't quite describe the peculiar feeling that crept through her, but it bore an uncomfortable resemblance to guilt. Or was it shame?

"And you thought I'd do something like that, what Lily did?" she whispered.

He shrugged and made no reply.

"Because I never would," she added vehemently.

"I think I knew that," he said quietly. "The fact that you didn't immediately take Lily's side and assume that Rusty had to be guilty, more or less confirms it."

He cupped her chin in his hand, then slid his fingers down her throat. Gazing into her face at her expressive eyes shining with sincerity, he thought of how young she was, how lovely and classy and sweet and vulnerable. He wanted her. He shouldn't, he didn't want to, but he did.

He loosed a troubled sigh. "I've never been attracted to the highborn ladies of Whitneyville," he told her, reminding himself as well. "Not even when I was a rebellious young buck out looking for trouble."

"I guess there have always been plenty of women who'll gladly give you what you want, so why bother with those stuck-up Whitneyville snobs," she said with a shaky laugh. It was probably the most risqué sentence she'd ever uttered in her entire life.

He laughed silently. "Something like that."

The vivid memory of his hot necking session with Penny Sherwood sprang instantly to Cheyenne's mind. And that had taken place in school! She couldn't even imagine what his extracurricular sex life had been like. Was still like! Her cheeks flamed.

His thumb drifted lazily up and down her neck. The fingers of his other hand strummed along her spine. "And suddenly," he murmured, "here I am, in the middle of the woods with the town princess, a hallowed widow yet!" He shook his head, his expression grim. "Maybe I'm an even bigger idiot than Cousin Rusty."

"I'm not," she said. Her voice was submissively soft. "And you're not."

Shivers coursed through her. She arched her neck into his touch, achingly aware of her body pressed against his. A hot coil of desire, the force of which she had never experienced, spiraled inside her abdomen. She wanted to feel his mouth on hers, to taste him. She wanted it overwhelmingly.

He continued to caress her neck and her back, but he made no move to kiss her. Heat swept through her. Somehow she felt both limp and tense, and her fingers tightened around the cloth of his shirt. Her breathing became shallow and swift. Her need was so deep, she threw off all the caution and convention that had been carefully instilled in her.

"If you ask me if I want you to kiss me, I'll say yes," she murmured huskily. She knew she should be shocked by her boldness, but she pushed it from her mind. She'd deal with it later. For the first time in her life, she knew the feeling of living strictly for the moment.

Caleb smiled and lowered his head. His lips brushed hers, slowly, sensuously. "Will you?"

"Yes," she breathed, not knowing what question she was answering. And not caring. Her arms went around his neck.

Three

Caleb's mouth came down on hers, hard, hot, and hungry. Cheyenne's lips parted instantly under the sensual onslaught, and his tongue penetrated and probed her mouth in breathtaking sexual stimulation.

She trembled and clung to him, her head spinning as if she were whirling and twirling on a dizzying carnival ride. She was twenty-eight years old, married and widowed, the mother of two, yet she had never experienced anything like the deep, rough, and demanding kiss she was sharing with Caleb Strong.

She couldn't remember ever feeling this hunger, this fire that raged through her. His heat and his hardness made her ache, and she responded to him with every part of her body. Her breasts felt full and ripe, and a honeyed warmth flowed between her legs.

Mindlessly, she strained up and into him, her hips rocking suggestively in a primal feminine rhythm that incited them both to greater passion. Their tongues rubbed sensuously as the tempestuous kiss grew longer, deeper, wetter.

Caleb's hands roamed over her, learning her shape, exploring the curves concealed beneath her loose-fitting dress. His fingers kneaded the hollow of her waist, smoothed over her hips, then cupped the rounded firmness of her bottom. His body was hard with tension. The pounding, urgent throb of desire blocked out all and any coherent thought.

He cupped her breasts and found them pleasingly full, larger than the shapeless dress revealed. She moaned when he flicked his thumbs over her nipples, and he did it again and again, while she writhed against him. He could feel the taut buds straining against the cloth barrier. He wanted to see them, taste them.

He lifted his mouth from hers, and as they both panted for breath, he kissed her temple, her cheeks, her ear. She felt his lips against the curve of her neck, then his tongue and the nip of his teeth. She gave a little cry at the dart of pleasure-pain, feeling as if she were drowning, losing herself in the swirling, blurring mists of passion.

"Damn, I wish we were naked," Caleb muttered. Frustration at not being able to touch her the way he wanted, or to see her or lie with her, gripped him. These restrictions of time and place fell into the realm of feverish adolescent groping, not adult sexuality. "I wish we were in bed!"

He had just verbalized what she was feeling, Cheyenne realized. They were thoughts she'd never had before. She had always assumed that she was too inhibited and repressed ever to feel the urges that inspired such longing. She had accepted long ago that she was sexually cold, incapable of passion. It was a stunning and darkly thrilling revelation to be proven wrong.

She pressed her forehead against his chest, sliding her arms around his waist. She couldn't make herself let go of him, though she knew the rules of propriety and decorum decreed that she must.

Closing her eyes, she realized that what she *wanted* to do had never been in such sharp conflict with what she *should* do. She had always been the "good girl," then the "respectable lady" who did exactly what she should.

Caleb felt her trembling in his arms and was astonished by the unexpected wave of tenderness he felt toward her. Reflexively, he stroked her silky hair, then kissed the top of her head. She murmured a small, inarticulate sound and cuddled closer.

For the first time in many years, he was nonplussed. He was holding the socially elite Cheyenne Whitney in his arms. She hadn't run screaming from him when he'd kissed her or acted like an outraged paragon, berating him for daring to touch her. He realized now that he had expected her to do any or all of those things, yet had decided to risk it anyway. He was nothing if not a risk taker.

He hadn't counted on her sweet acquiescence and voluptuous response to him, though. Nor had he anticipated the powerful desire he felt for her. It was dangerous, too alluring, and unsettling enough to make a daredevil like himself begin to view certain risks conservatively.

He was too perceptive to confuse lust with desire. Lust, he was familiar with. That swift, seething hormonal surge, which could be acted upon and then forgotten, was not what he felt for Cheyenne. The desire he felt for her was something else entirely. It turned a stolen kiss in the woods into a mind-blowing moment of truth. It touched him deep inside, making him feel as if he had crossed some invisible line, irrevocably changing himself.

Was he crazy? What was he getting himself into? As a rebel and a risk taker, he seldom experienced panic, but he felt on the verge of it now. The last thing he needed in his life was a complication like Cheyenne Whitney! The timing couldn't be worse. And she was wrong for him, all wrong. He despised Whitneyville, he couldn't remember when he hadn't, and she practically embodied the town.

He dropped his arms and moved away from her.

"Look, that . . . uh, went further than I'd intended."

"That's funny." She looked at the ground and shoved her hands deep into the pockets of her dress. "I thought you'd say it didn't go far enough."

Cheyenne was astonished at her brazen frankness. The violent needs and emotions churning through her had unleashed something else inside her, something that made it impossible for her to remain passively silent.

Caleb almost smiled. Instead he forced a scowl. "You're way out of your league with me, little girl. You'd better run back to your—"

"I can't go anywhere until I catch my dog," she interrupted prosaically. She knew what he'd been about to say. *Run back to your safe little world.* He was rejecting her, and she didn't think she could stand to hear the words.

"You don't have to stay, though," she added quietly. "I'll find him and take him home."

Caleb's scowl deepened. She wasn't going to throw a tantrum or beg him to stay with her. She was inviting him to leave, and being gracious about it too. Perversely, having been granted his escape, he didn't want to go.

"I can't leave you out here alone in the middle of this . . . park? Woods? Whatever the hell this place is," he snapped.

"I'll be fine, really. I walk Peppy here every night. On his leash, of course." She turned and walked swiftly to the middle of the low stone bridge that spanned Silver Creek. "Peppy, come here!"

Caleb followed her. "There he is."

"Where?"

"Over there, to your left." She turned her head in the direction his finger was pointing, but he knew she still didn't see the dog. Automatically, he cupped the side of her face with his hand and aimed her line of vision to the large oak where the irrepressible Peppy was lurking. "See?"

She nodded. His hand was strong and warm against her cheek. Unaccountably, tears filled her eyes. "Yes, I see. Thank you." She stumbled blindly from the bridge to the sandy bank. "Come on, Peppy," she coaxed.

Peppy barked and charged into the fast-flowing waters of the creek. It was less than a foot deep, but his running leaps splashed water everywhere. Bounding out of the stream, the dog launched himself at Cheyenne. He stood on his back legs and used his two wet, dirty front paws to support himself against her chest.

Cheyenne grabbed the sodden leash, which had become entwined between them. The sudden movement threw them both off balance, and they tumbled to the ground.

Caleb raced from the bridge. Cheyenne was lying on her side, one arm and one leg firmly wrapped around the wriggling, muddy, wet dog, who suddenly gave her cheek a generous swipe with his tongue.

"Oh, stop!" She was laughing and holding on to the dog and trying to shield her face from his devoted ministrations, all at the same time. "Get up, you idiot. You're the worst dog. You're a crazy dog."

Her laughter, filled with affection, belied her words—and hit Caleb with the force of an emotional tidal wave. No whining or screaming for her, no harsh reprimands or hitting the animal for getting her dirty. She looked like a carefree girl playing with her dog. Her deep, rich laugh affected him like the most intimate caress.

"You're both crazy." His voice was husky, and Caleb was aware that he sounded more admiring than admonishing. He slipped his hands under her arms and lifted her to her feet with one easy sweep.

"Thank you," she said softly. She clutched Peppy's leash with one hand and tried to smooth her disheveled hair with the other.

His gaze flicked over her. "Get on the back of the bike and I'll ride you home. Keep hold of the leash, and we'll go slow enough for the dog to walk alongside us."

"I'd better not. I'll get you all wet and muddy too."

An innocent statement, certainly not provocative, yet Caleb felt heat rise in him, swelling his already-aching loins. "Just get on the bike and stop arguing," he said tightly.

He matched the motorcycle's speed to the dog's pace, going so slowly that Cheyenne, seated behind him, didn't have to hold on to him for balance. She clutched the back of his seat with one hand instead, keeping a firm grip on Peppy's leash with the other.

He pulled in front of 100 Silver Creek Road, and she hopped off the bike. "Thank you for the ride and for helping to find Peppy," she said quickly. She took great care not to look at him.

It was his cue to ride off into the night, Caleb thought. The fact that he was so reluctant to leave her made it imperative that he do just that. "It's too late for me to visit Joni Lynn tonight," he said gruffly. "Tell her I'll see her tomorrow."

"Yes, I'll tell her." Cheyenne stared down at the damp splotches and muddy paw prints covering her thoroughly wrinkled dress. She didn't even want to guess what her hair must've looked like. There was no getting around it, she was a mess.

Oddly enough, her uncharacteristic lapse in neatness provided her with a bravado she normally didn't possess. It was as if someone else were masquerading as Cheyenne Whitney Merrit, some wild hoyden who would do all the things that her exemplary alter ego never could.

Things like extending an invitation to Caleb Strong. "You're welcome to come to dinner tomorrow if you'd like to visit Joni Lynn then," she heard herself say.

"Dinner tomorrow?" he repeated. "Here, at your house?" He sounded incredulous.

"I'm not a bad cook." She marveled at the ease with

which this alien Cheyenne teased him. "Nobody has died of food poisoning from one of my meals yet." Why, she was even making jokes!

Her smile entranced him. Her beautifully shaped lips and perfect white teeth, the small dimple indenting her left cheek . . . He remembered the way they'd kissed, how hot and sweet her mouth had felt under his, her unconditionally passionate response to him. . . .

He fully intended to refuse her invitation to dinner. There was really no point in carrying this impossible little dalliance any further.

"Okay," he said. "What time?" He stared at the ground, momentarily disconcerted. He'd said the opposite of what he'd planned! Rarely did his tongue betray him. However outrageous or spontaneous his remarks might seem, all were calculated to achieve the effect he sought.

Cheyenne smiled her relief. It would've hurt if he had refused, she realized. "Is six too early? The children get hungry if—"

"Six is fine." Her kids would be there, he reminded himself. His niece would be there. They would eat dinner, then he would leave. There would be nothing more to it than that. "See you tomorrow."

He gunned the engine and roared off into the night. Cheyenne stood at the gate of her white picket fence and stared into the darkness for a long time after he'd gone. Not until her pulse rate had returned to normal, her skin had cooled, and the throbbing upheaval inside her had quieted, did she enter the house.

The talk in the teachers' lounge the next day centered almost entirely on the Whitneyville Chamber of Commerce's loss to the Dix-Mart chain. The corporation which built, owned, and ran fifteen hundred giant discount stores in thirty-one states, had bought a large parcel of land four years earlier on the outskirts of Whitneyville. The chamber had launched a series of court fights to prevent Dix-Mart from building. The battle had lasted until the previous day, finally resulting in victory for Dix-Mart.

"It was all for nothing," Allison Hinton, the high school's history teacher, said bitterly. "Now Dix-Mart will come into Whitneyville and build their Discount City and drive all the downtown retailers out of business."

Allison's father, Roy, owned Hinton's Pharmacy in town, and had been one of the leaders in the fight against the dreaded Dix-Mart encroachment. "It's happened in town after town," she continued. "Dix-Mart moves into small communities like Whitneyville, and overnight the customers' buying patterns change from downtown to Dix-Mart!"

"Who can compete with them?" Larry Flanagan, the physics teacher, said with a sigh. "They buy in volume so they can undercut everybody in price."

"On the other hand, they do provide lots of jobs," Archer Byron, the football coach, pointed out. "And think of the taxes and utility payments a place that size will bring in. It'll pump more money into the local economy." He brightened visibly. "I also heard that Dix-Mart company policy is to support the local community programs. Like the Boosters Club supports the football team."

"It seems that we have a Benedict Arnold right here in our midst," Allison said angrily. "Boosters Club, indeed! Don't you have any loyalty to the town, Archer? Every small business in Whitneyville is facing economic ruin, and you talk about what the enemy can do for you."

Cheyenne stepped into the fray, assuming the role of peacemaker. "I read somewhere that there are consulting firms that actually specialize in advising small-town businesses on how to handle the arrival of a Dix-mart. Do you suppose the chamber could hire one of them to—"

"—to tell us to face the inevitable?" Allison cut in. She didn't care for peace, not in this war. She turned her attention to the home ec teacher. "Joyce, your sister Lindsay is co-owner of the craft shop in town. How does she feel about Dix-Mart coming?"

"Terrible," Joyce said grimly. "Dix-Mart can stock three times as many materials and charge much less for them. It's like David facing Goliath—and losing!"

"It's a crisis that will affect everybody in town," Dawn Bentley told Cheyenne, Martha Mayfield, Deborah Winston, and Polly Maitland later that afternoon as they stood in the aisle of Bentley's Five-and-Dime.

The store, which carried a vast array of merchandise, from toys and cosmetics to clothes and candy, had been in the Bentley family for four generations. Dawn, a high school classmate of Cheyenne's, had married into the Bentley family and felt as possessive of the store as anyone born Bentley.

"Our main competition has been Hinton's Pharmacy," Dawn continued in a low, rapid voice, "and we certainly weren't pleased when they branched out from drugs and medical supplies to gift items, cards, and makeup—definitely our type of stock. But at least, well, the Hintons are—"

She broke off abruptly as the big glass doors to the five-and-dime swooshed open, and over a dozen noisy, boisterous children pushed their way inside. Dawn grimaced. "Excuse me, ladies. I have to handle this *horde*." She glared disapprovingly at the children, as if they were indeed a horde of barbarian invaders.

Cheyenne automatically stepped closer to the candy counter where her six-year-old Brittany and five-year-old Jeffrey were carefully making their selections.

"Let's get these and go home," she suggested, handing each child a pack of sugarless gum. She laid a protective hand on their shoulders as the young gang jostled their way through the narrow aisles, heading directly toward the candy.

"Children!" Dawn said sharply. "We have rules here. No more than two children who are unaccompanied by an adult are allowed in the store at the same time. All but two of you will have to leave and wait your turn outside."

"No problem, sister." A lazy, mocking male voice sounded above the din as Caleb Strong sauntered into the store. "The kids aren't unaccompanied. They're all with me. Nieces, nephews, cousins, and a neighborhood kid or two."

Cheyenne's heart slammed against her ribs at the sight of him, and her gaze lingered helplessly on his roughishly handsome face. His eyes were so blue, and his mouth . . . Oh, his mouth. Quaking inwardly, she told herself to look away from him. Instead her eyes lowered to study the rest of him.

He was wearing low-slung faded blue jeans that fit his hips and legs in a most sex-defining way. She stared at his powerful, hard thighs and the sizable bulge between them, and her mouth suddenly went dry. His navy T-shirt adhered to the muscular breadth of his chest, and he had rolled up the sleeves so that the cobra tattoo was plainly visible.

Cheyenne saw Dawn eye the cobra, then immediately retreat behind the counter. "We will not tolerate rowdy behavior in the store," she announced imperiously.

"Good policy," Caleb said. He strode toward the children who were swarming over the candy counter, snatching, grabbing, and laughing.

"Hey, kids, you have to be real quiet in here." He swooped a little girl of about three up into his arms. "No talking, no laughing, no having fun. So pick out what you want and we'll get out of here. Things will be different when the new Dix-Mart opens," he added, his eyes gleaming. His voice was just loud enough to carry beyond the group of children to Dawn Bentley, who was seething behind the counter. "They like kids in Dix-Mart, you know. They like all their customers. Having Dix-Mart move in is going to be the best thing that's ever happened to this town."

It was undoubtedly the worst thing he could have said, given the time, place, and circumstances, and Cheyenne knew he'd planned it that way. Martha Mayfield, Deborah Winston, and Polly Maitland all gasped disapprovingly and sent him condemning glares. Cheyenne saw Dawn lean across the counter to whisper something to the Misses Creighton, who were purchasing their monthly supply of paperback books.

Caleb noticed too. "Dix-Mart has a book department at least twice this size, and they get their shipments earlier," he said to the two elderly sisters. "They give a nice discount on each book too. You'll save a bundle."

The Creighton sisters looked pleased. Dawn Bentley looked homicidal.

"I wanna go to Dix-Mart, Uncle Caleb," shouted one of the little boys.

"Soon, Matthew." Caleb smiled broadly. "By next spring the Dix-Mart will be open for business. Of course, Bentley's Five-and-Dime might be closing shortly afterward."

There was a fierce, offended "tsk" from Polly Maitland. Cheyenne glanced nervously from Dawn's infuriated face to Caleb's mocking one. Her eyes collided with his, and he noticed her standing there for the first time.

The sight of her affected him viscerally. She'd been appealing enough the night before in that baggy dress with no makeup and tousled hair. This afternoon, with her makeup in place, her ash-blond hair shiny and full and tumbling around her shoulders, her pencil-slim, cream-colored skirt and peach silk blouse enhancing her curvy shapeliness, she was a knockout.

And she was a lady, he reminded himself. A classy, wellborn Whiteneyville lady who would never challenge convention by fraternizing with a Strong. At night, alone in the dark was one thing, public recognition was another. He waited for her inevitable snub.

Cheyenne realized she was holding her breath. If he made some snide reference to their tryst in the woods, or mentioned that he was due at her house for dinner in two and a half hours, the news would flash through Whitneyville like a message on a telegraph. Her reputation . . .

She nervously moistened her lips. Caleb looked as compellingly masculine and wickedly virile as he had last night, perhaps even more so. There had been a fantasylike aspect to that adventure in the dark woods. Today, in the middle of the afternoon in the middle of town, the fantasy element was gone. Caleb Strong was very real.

And he was looking at her, his brows arched, his mouth twisted in a sardonic smile.

He didn't expect her to speak to him! The flash of insight penetrated her with piercing clarity. Her fingers flexed against her children's small shoulders, and she drew a deep, bolstering breath.

"Hello, Caleb," she said softly. She saw the surprise flash in his eyes and knew she'd been right. He hadn't believed she would acknowledge him.

Caleb nodded curtly but said nothing. This was one of the few times in his life when he had no glib, ready response. He hadn't expected her to acknowledge him. Her quiet hello had astonished him, and he was seldom astonished by anyone or anything.

"Are they your kids?" he asked gruffly, glancing down at Brittany and Jeffrey. The little girl was slightly built with large hazel eyes like her mother's and beribboned blond braids that hung past her shoulders. The boy was as tall as his sister and huskier, his eyes and hair a shade darker.

Cheyenne nodded. "Yes. This is Brittany and Jeffrey. Say hello to Mr. Strong," she instructed them.

She heard Martha Mayfield's sharp intake of breath, saw Polly Maitland arch her eyebrows and mouth "Strong" to Deborah Winston.

"Hello, Mr. Strong," Brittany said obediently.

Jeffrey was too busy staring at the gang of children. Each child had chosen a one-pound bag of candy, the size that Cheyenne purchased only at Halloween for trick-or-treaters. The little boy glanced down at the single pack of sugarless gum in his hand and frowned.

"I want that," he said, pointing to the bag of Snickers bars a boy his age was clutching.

"Melanie, give the kid a bag like that," Caleb said to a little girl who looked about eight years old. The child complied, handing Jeffrey a big bag of Snickers.

Looking thrilled, Jeffrey dropped the gum and clutched his treasure.

"Jeffrey," Cheyenne began, "you can't have—"

"It's mine!" he yelled, running away from her and slipping into the midst of the Strong children. His plan clearly was to seek anonymity among them.

"Hiding in plain sight," Caleb said, grinning and obviously amused by the boy's antics. "Do you want some candy, too, Brittany?" he asked the little girl. "My treat."

Brittany looked uncertainly at her mother.

Cheyenne shook her head no. "It's very kind of you to offer, but we really can't accept." Her eyes widened with dismay as she saw Jeffrey follow the giggling pack of children toward the toy department in the back of the store. "Jeffrey, come here," she called.

Her son didn't even glance her way.

Caleb chuckled. "You don't really expect him to

hand over the candy and meekly follow you out, do
you?"

"I certainly do," she said firmly. She glanced at her
watch. "I have to leave now and—"

"Let him stay with us," Caleb cut in. "I'll drop him
by"—he paused—"later."

Both were aware that he could have mentioned the
dinner, thus alerting all the eavesdropping bystand-
ers. Both were aware that he hadn't, and why.

"Oh, no, I couldn't possibly impose on you," Cheyenne said hastily. "I'll just get him and bring him
home with me."

"Uncle Caleb!" A little girl around seven years old
came shrieking up the aisle toward them. "They're
here! The New Kids dolls. Can I get one, please?
Please, please, please," she added for good measure,
grabbing his arm and hugging it to her.

The little girl thrust a box in Caleb's hand. Cheyenne noted that the doll inside was dressed like a
biker in faux black leather, and wore an earring in
his plastic ear. Her gaze shifted to the little girl. She
was missing two front teeth and wore a small-size
version of an outfit similar to those Cheyenne had
seen certain high school girls wear. She didn't care
for the slightly trashy style for the teenagers, no
matter how trendy, and she certainly didn't approve
of it on a seven-year-old.

She looked at Brittany, so precious and appropri-
ately little girlish in her blue-smocked dress and
white lacy socks and black patent leather strapped
shoes. Why, she wondered, would any mother dress
her child like a miniature hooker? No wonder the
youngster wanted to play with biker dolls!

Caleb smiled indulgently at the girl. "What have
you got here, Kimmy? New Kids On The Block,
hmm?" He examined the doll.

"He's gonna be Barbie's new boyfriend if you buy
him, Uncle Caleb." Kimmy jumped up and down
excitedly.

"He looks pretty tough for Barbie. Think she can handle him?"

"Yes, yes!" Kimmy cried. Unexpectedly, she turned to Brittany, who was watching her avidly. "Jordan's my favorite New Kid. Who's yours?"

"I like Jonathan," Brittany said shyly.

Cheyenne was stunned that Brittany even knew what Kimmy was talking about. She herself was vaguely aware of the New Kids On The Block singing group, but she certainly didn't expect little Brittany to know a thing about rock groups or be able to name the individuals in one!

"They have Jonathan back there!" Kimmy exclaimed. "My cousin Melanie got him and there's one left. C'mon!" She tucked her doll under one arm and grabbed Brittany's hand.

To Cheyenne's utter amazement, Brittany—her timid, cautious, shy Brittany—raced off with Kimmy without a single backward glance. "I . . . uh, I'll go and get them," she mumbled to no on in particular, and hurried toward the toy section.

She'd been excruciatingly aware of the curiosity and disapproval that was emanating from her Whitneyville peers, and it was a relief to escape from their unrelenting stares. But then she winced with dismay at the sight that greeted her in the toy aisle.

A plethora of young male Strongs was crowding the racks where small cars, trucks, turtle figures in martial arts garb, and an alarming assortment of plastic assault weapons were displayed. The toys were placed high and out of reach, so the children were climbing up on the shelves to reach them. Jeffrey stood on the second shelf, waving a facsimile of a gun that Cheyenne had seen in a news clip of a drug war shoot-out.

"Jeffrey!" She was appalled by the gun and by her son's perch, four feet above the ground.

"Bad marketing display," she heard Caleb say. He had followed her and stood directly behind her. "The toys should be placed at the kids' eye level, and the merchandise should be within their reach."

He strode over and plucked Jeffrey and another boy off the shelves. "Stay on the ground, okay, Matthew, Jeffrey? I know we'd have the makings of a terrific lawsuit against Bentley's if you fell and got hurt, but we don't want to waste all that time in court, do we? And who likes hospital emergency rooms anyway?"

"Yeah," both little boys agreed cheerfully. To what they were agreeing, Cheyenne wasn't sure. She was positive, though, that no one had ever before talked of lawsuits and emergency rooms to Jeffrey.

Before she could retrieve her son, her attention was drawn farther down the aisle to where the little girls had gathered. There was Brittany, sitting on the floor— the dirty, old-styled wooden floor!—surrounded by a group of girls, all of whom were opening boxes of dolls and oohing and aahing over them.

"Brittany!" she gasped. She had never permitted her children to open any item until it was paid for and they'd left the store, not even when they'd been toddlers, demanding a cookie from the box of Arrow-root biscuits tucked in the supermarket cart. But there was her daughter, smiling and chatting as she held up a male doll dressed as disreputably as Kimmy's black leather biker. Its box lay discarded beside her.

Cheyenne was speechless. It crossed her mind that her carefully raised children had spent less than ten minutes in the company of the Strongs and had already been corrupted by them. She turned abruptly and crashed into the big, muscular frame of Caleb Strong. The impact left her momentarily breathless.

He placed his hands on her shoulders, ostensibly to steady her. But the sexy, smoldering look in his eyes revealed an altogether different reason.

She gazed up at him. Her breathlessness persisted, but was no longer the result of their collision.

Four

"Whoa!" Caleb laughed huskily. "Careful, Miss Cheyenne." His voice flowed over her like warm honey, and
his wicked smile challenged her. It aroused her too.

She was aware of a shameful urge to lean into him,
to feel the unyielding planes of his body pressed
tightly against her. As they had last night. . . . A
host of wanton memories washed over her, and the
effects were profoundly physical. Her breasts swelled,
the tips taut and tingling. Between her thighs . . .
she couldn't suppress the whimper that escaped from
her throat.

Caleb heard the small, sensuous sound, and his
knowing smile widened. He slid his hands down her
arms until he reached her hands, then caught them
in his, interlocking their fingers. "Are we taking the
dog for another walk tonight?" he asked, his voice
deep and low and seductive. His eyes were gleaming.

Cheyenne knew he knew exactly what she'd been
thinking and feeling and wanting. . . .

Her face flaming, she swiftly stepped back, pulling
her hands from his. Brittany and Jeffrey weren't the
only ones to have succumbed to the powerful allure of
the Strongs, she acknowledged ruefully. Summoning
her considerable self-control, she put a brake on her

runaway thoughts and forced herself to confront the problems at hand.

"Caleb, the children are trashing the store. They've torn into the toys and are—"

"Relax. I'm buying the stuff. I told them each to pick out the toy they want. What they've opened, they'll be taking home."

Her jaw dropped as she surveyed the number of children and toys. "You're buying all those toys?" she asked incredulously. How in the world could he afford such largess?

"Don't worry, Miss Cheyenne, I can pay," he said caustically. He withdrew a roll of bills from the pocket of his jeans. She saw twenties, fifties, one hundred-dollar bills. "I'm not gonna stiff your friends, the Bentleys."

Her cheeks pinkened. "I didn't mean to imply—"

"Sure you did. And now you can start wondering how I happen to have this much cash on me. Maybe I knocked over a bank on my way back to Whitneyville? Or maybe I hit it big at the track and these are my winnings? Or won the Florida state lottery? Choose whichever one you want."

To be fair, Caleb admitted that he, too, would be suspicious of a character with no known job history or visible means of support, who blew into town flashing a thick roll of big bills. But he had no intention of using any of his credit cards in Whitneyville. When he returned to his myopic hometown, he acted the part he had been assigned since birth. While in Whitneyville, he was the loser-misfit everyone expected him to be, and he took satisfaction in not letting them know otherwise.

He looked at Cheyenne whose expressive face was reflecting her varying states of confusion, disapproval, anxiety . . . and desire. She was attracted to him, he knew, and as difficult as it was for him to accept, he wanted her too. But their mutual attraction couldn't bridge the enormous gap between them. In Whitneyville, his us-against-them mentality was in full operation, and Cheyenne Whitney Merrit was definitely one of "them."

He turned to the swarm of children. "Hey, kids, does everybody have something?" There was a happy affirmative chorus. "Then head to the check-out counter at the front of the store."

The children obliged in an immediate stampede. Brittany nimbly escaped with the Strongs, but Cheyenne managed to catch Jeffrey as he started off with the sinister toy gun. "Jeffrey, put that back," she ordered.

"Uncle Caleb said we could have whatever we wanted," piped up the little boy named Matthew, who'd stuck close to Jeffrey's side.

"Uncle Caleb said I could have it!" Jeffrey wailed.

"Jeffrey, Mr. Strong is not your uncle and—"

"He's not Derrick's uncle either," Matthew interrupted, "but Derrick is getting the Teenage Mutant Ninja Turtles Sewer Playset. See?" He pointed to a small boy struggling to carry a tall, colorful box to the front of the store. "Uncle Caleb likes to buy stuff for kids," Matthew added knowledgeably.

"That's right, Matthew," Caleb said. "Now, you take your toy and your candy and line up at the check-out with the others."

Matthew trotted off. Caleb turned to Cheyenne and Jeffrey, who was still gripping the gun. "What's the problem, Cheyenne?"

"What's the problem?" she repeated. "I don't know where to start. First, I—"

"Mommy doesn't like guns!" Jeffrey burst out. He was on the verge of tears. "I want this gun, Uncle Caleb."

"Uh-oh." Caleb rolled his eyes. "A classic case of pacifist mom and weapon-crazy kid clashing in the aisle of the toy department."

"It's not funny, Caleb," Cheyenne said seriously. "I don't want my child playing with a replica of a monstrous death machine. And then there is the matter of you spending your"—she paused and cleared her throat—"your hard-earned money on my children, whom you didn't meet until ten minutes ago."

"Okay, okay. One thing at a time." He got down on his haunches, eye level with Jeffrey. "Jeffrey, if you could have anything in this store besides this gun, what would you want? You tell me and I'll buy it for you."

"Caleb," Cheyenne began. "You can't—"

He ignored her. "Name it, Jeffrey."

"The Teenage Mutant Ninja Turtles Sewer Playset!" Jeffrey shrieked, dropping the gun. "I have four turtles but they don't have anyplace to live."

"Jeffrey!" Cheyenne was genuinely distressed. The abode in question was a big toy that cost too much, the kind she only purchased for birthdays or Christmas when she broke her budget and painfully over-extended herself. She couldn't permit Caleb Strong to buy it for Jeffrey, although by refusing, she was casting herself in the role of heartless heavy.

"We can't have those turtles going homeless." Caleb picked up Jeffrey and carried him to the toy display, where he removed the boxed set from the shelf. "The sewer it is."

Stupefied with joy, Jeffrey wrapped his arms around the box, smiling as Caleb strode off with him. Cheyenne had no choice but to trail after them. Her insides were churning. She felt almost disoriented by the emotions coursing through her. Caleb's generosity was as unexpected as it was unsettling. What should she do? She hadn't a clue. There had never been anyone who had offered to treat her children to extravagant presents on the spur of the moment.

Her widowed mother, living frugally in Arizona, sent gifts of clothing on the appropriate occasions. Evan's parents, retired and living in Texas, did the same. Evan's brother, Hunter, and his wife, Janelle, who lived in Whitneyville with their own two children, had elected to eliminate family presents altogether.

But now here was Caleb Strong. . . .

They approached the check-out, and Cheyenne was shocked to hear Dawn Bentley lambasting the children, who had lined up with their prizes. She looked at Brittany, clutching her new doll as she stood sandwiched between two other little girls. The Strong girls seemed impervious to Dawn's vicious tone, but Brittany's hazel eyes were round as saucers as the woman ranted on, threatening to evict them all from the store and accusing them of vandalism and shoplifting. No one had ever spoken so harshly to Brittany Whitney Merrit in her entire short life.

The Strongs, right down to the littlest one, didn't budge an inch. "Uncle Caleb is coming, he'll take care of everything," one of the older boys said confidently.

And there he was, right on cue. "Haven't you started ringing up this stuff yet?" Caleb asked the teenage cashier. She was cowering behind the register, seemingly as unnerved by Dawn's diatribe as Brittany was. He set Jeffrey's toy on the counter, and the girl hesitantly reached for it.

"This isn't a charitable distribution center," Dawn snapped, stepping in front of the girl. "Someone has to pay for all this!"

Cheyenne cringed. She was seeing the character of her longtime friend in a whole new light, and it illuminated a disturbing lack of kindness.

"I'm paying for everything," Caleb replied with a chilling smile. "This is the biggest sale you're going to have until the Christmas season, so I suggest you let the girl here start ringing it up. Go ahead, honey," he said to the young cashier. "You're doing fine. Don't let Mrs. Bentley's evil tongue scare you."

"Yeah, she's always mean," one of the boys said matter-of-factly. "She's always yelling at us."

At that moment, Brittany spied her mother and ran to her. She threw her small arms around Cheyenne's legs, clinging to her. "Mommy, she said the police were going to come and take us to jail!" the

little girl sobbed. She was shaking and clearly terrified.

As Cheyenne picked her up, rage poured through
her. She carried Brittany to the counter, where Dawn
stared at her in sudden horrified embarrassment.

"You threatened my child and scared her half to
death," Cheyenne said icily.

"Cheyenne," Dawn began, "I didn't know your little
Brittany was—"

"I heard the way you were talking to all the children," Cheyenne interrupted. "It was disgusting and
inexcusable. How could you speak to anyone in such
a vitriolic manner, let alone young children? I believe
you owe each of them—and Mr. Strong as well—an
apology."

Dawn's face was mottled and purple, her lips pulled
into a taut, thin line. "Cheyenne, I am sorry if
Brittany was upset," she said through gritted teeth.
She glanced at Caleb and the line of young Strongs,
then abruptly fled from the store.

"Well, that was an apology of sorts, from a Bentley
to a Whitney," Caleb said, shrugging nonchalantly.
"Obviously, the thought of apologizing to a Strong
was too much for her to handle."

The young cashier smiled as she began to ring up
the purchases. "Mrs. Merrit, you were terrific," she
said. Cheyenne recognized the girl then as one of her
past students. "Mrs. Bentley is so nasty to the little
kids who come in here, unless, of course, they're with
people like you. Then she sucks up to them. If I didn't
need this job, I'd quit today."

"Apply to Dix-Mart when it opens in the spring,"
Caleb suggested. "Better pay, better opportunities,
and no Bentleys."

The girl laughed appreciatively.

At last, all the purchases were rung up and bagged,
and the children followed Caleb outside. Cheyenne
walked beside him. Jeffrey and Brittany were in the
middle of the throng, their presents firmly in hand.
The whole group walked toward the bus stop, which

was on the way to the lot where Cheyenne's car was parked.

"Caleb, I want to thank you," she said.

"You don't have to," he said abruptly. "Brittany and Jeffrey already have, several times."

"They are overwhelmed," she said. "They've never been part of a toy-buying spree before. I wasn't going to let you buy them anything," she added. "But after that awful scene with Dawn . . ." She gulped. She was still upset by it.

Caleb's eyes gleamed. "I was amazed by that scene. Proper little Cheyenne losing her temper and tearing into a Whitneyville peer? And in public yet! I ask you, what's this town coming to?"

Cheyenne stared at the ground. "I was ashamed of the way Dawn behaved," she confessed softly. "She was so terrible to the children—and so rude to you. And when Brittany started to cry and I realized how frightened she was, I . . ." Her voice trailed off.

Caleb had said it all, she thought. She'd lost her temper and ripped into Dawn—and in full public view. Definitely a first in the life of Cheyenne Whitney Merrit.

"You reminded me of a mother lion whose cub had been threatened," he said. He flashed that heart-stopping, teasing grin of his. "I liked your fighting spirit. It was unexpected. And defending the other kids and me was certainly exceptional. No one ever bothers to take a Strong's side in this town."

"If that's a sample of the way you and your family have been treated, I don't blame you for hating Whitneyville."

"I've urged the family to leave and settle somewhere else. They don't want to go. It's home to them. They like living down by the river, close to one another. Not even my cousin Rusty wanted to leave after the Lily Thurman mess. He's still here, living with his mother and working at Wheaton's Gas Station." Caleb shrugged. "Go figure."

They reached the bus stop, and Caleb shepherded the children around him.

"I can't believe you single-handedly brought fifteen children shopping on the bus," Cheyenne murmured, staring at him and the mob of talking, laughing children. It was a feat she knew she would never attempt. "It was extremely brave of you."

"Or extremely stupid," he said carelessly. "How else were we going to get here?"

How, indeed, she mused. But who else would even consider taking fifteen kids on a crowded, smelly bus to buy them toys and candy? It was plain to see Caleb was at ease with the children, that he enjoyed them. She gazed at him, and a fierce emotion surged through her. From his tattoo, his motorcycle, his laughing air of indifference, to the devil gleam in his blue eyes and his hot, hard mouth, she'd never known anyone like him in her life.

He arched his brows quizzically, and she realized she was staring at him. Flushing with embarrassment, she made a stab at recovering both her composure and her spinning thoughts. "I'd offer to drive you, but I have a little Ford Escort that's barely big enough for the three of us."

"That's okay, you'd need a school bus to transport this gang." He grinned, then turned to a small boy who was clamoring for his attention.

Cheyenne watched for a moment, until she felt Jeffrey tug at her hand. "This is heavy, Mom," he announced, handing her his cumbersome package.

"We'll . . . um, see you at six, Caleb?" she said softly.

He met her eyes. "Six," he confirmed.

"Isn't Cheyenne a good cook, Uncle Caleb?" Joni Lynn asked enthusiastically as she passed him the bowl of mashed potatoes. "We eat dinners like this every night here."

Caleb surveyed the dinner—fried chicken with

country gravy, mashed potatoes, green peas, sliced tomatoes, and freshly baked buttermilk biscuits. Joni Lynn had already informed him that there was peach cobbler, also made from scratch, for dessert.

It was home cooking at its finest, and he was enjoying every mouth-watering bite. He glanced sidelong at Cheyenne, who had changed into casual, dark green culottes and a matching sleeveless blouse.

The culotte skirt hugged her slim waist and was modestly cut, the hem only a few inches above her knee. But the sight of her shapely legs had transfixed him for a few disconcerting moments when he first arrived. Throughout dinner, too, his gaze kept wandering to her slender arms and the tantalizing slope of her shoulders. He struggled to get a grip on himself. Since when did he find *arms* and *shoulders* a turn-on? Since when did he merely look at a woman and find his body throbbing and hard?

Since encountering Cheyenne Whitney Merrit, that's when. He swallowed, hard.

"The peas and tomatoes are from the garden in the backyard," Joni Lynn continued happily. "Don't they taste better than the ones you buy at the store?"

"Everything is delicious. I'm impressed," he drawled. Never would he admit just how much. Instead, he took refuge in humor. "My mama and Joni Lynn's mama, that's my sister Crystal, have never been very talented in the kitchen. Our meals tended to come from a can and go directly to the plate."

"Sometimes they heat it up first," Joni Lynn put in, her eyes twinkling.

"Yeah. On holidays," Caleb added. He and Joni Lynn laughed.

Cheyenne smiled uncertainly. They were joking, weren't they? Sometimes it was hard to tell with Caleb. Joni Lynn, quiet and serious-minded, had rarely mentioned her family before, but now she was kidding playfully with her uncle, seemingly quite comfortable in his company.

Joni Lynn had been clearly astonished when Cheyenne had told her that her uncle was coming to dinner. She'd tried to sound casual about the invitation, as if having a Strong to dinner was something quite ordinary. As if inviting any man to dinner was an everyday occurrence in her life. Fortunately, Joni Lynn had refrained from making any comments.

She was making plenty of comments now, though, all of them highly complimentary. "Cheyenne also cooks breakfast," she said with a rapturous sigh. "Things like pancakes and waffles and eggs, any way you like them. I can't even remember the last time I had dry cereal for breakfast."

"I like to cook," Cheyenne said, shrugging. Joni Lynn's effusive praise was definitely becoming embarrassing. But she thrilled to the sight of Caleb savoring the meal. There was something so primally satisfying in cooking for him . . . in feeding her man. . . . The silent admission made her feel foolishly old-fashioned and stupidly romantic. Not to mention the obvious. Caleb Strong was *not* her man.

It was the most mundane of dinner table conversations, Caleb thought, with three kids and a dog present, yet a gripping sexual tension kept building inside him. He sought desperately to break it. After all, giving into it was not an option. He didn't dare, not after last night's explosive kiss. He'd lain awake half the night, feeling its effects.

"I feel as if I've stepped into a fifties sitcom," he said dryly. Nothing like humor, slightly edged, to lighten things up. "I didn't think anybody cooked Sunday-dinner-type meals every night. And I didn't realize that anyone cooked breakfast these days either. Except McDonald's, of course."

Jeffrey abruptly dropped his spoon and pushed his plate away. "Let's go to McDonald's and get a Happy Meal," he said eagerly.

"Not tonight, Jeffrey," Joni Lynn said, smiling. "We're eating our dinner right now."

Jeffrey's light brown eyes grew stormy. Caleb had

been around children often enough to know when a potential tantrum was brewing. "Tell you what, Jeffrey," he said. "Next time I take the kids to McDonald's, I'll stop by for you and Brittany. If your mom says it's okay, you can go with us."

"It's okay," Jeffrey assured him.

Cheyenne sent Caleb a grateful smile for his timely intervention. He smiled back, and for one sweet moment there was just the two of them, their gazes locked, their eyes warm.

Then reality interceded. Jeffrey spilled his milk and while Cheyenne was sponging it up, Brittany whispered urgently to Joni Lynn.

"Brittany wants to ask you something, Uncle Caleb," the girl said as Brittany fidgeted anxiously in her chair.

"Ask away, sweetheart," he said.

Cheyenne stared curiously at her daughter. What was Brittany up to? The child rarely initiated conversation with adults, but then Caleb was unlike any of the adults Brittany knew. He was something akin to Santa Claus. At that thought, Cheyenne tensed. Surely Brittany wasn't about to ask him for another doll? Mortified in advance, she prepared to admonish the girl for greediness.

"I want to play with Kimmy and Melanie," Brittany said shyly.

"They already told me they'd like to play with you too," Caleb said. "How about tomorrow after school? I'll drive you down to Kimmy's house. Melanie is always over there because her mom works till five." He glanced at Cheyenne who had frozen, the wet sponge in midair. "Of course, you'll have to ask your mother if it's all right with her," he added at once.

"Can I, Mommy?" Brittany pleaded. "Please!"

"May I?" Cheyenne corrected automatically. She felt uneasy. Send her child to play at the Strongs? She fervently wished Brittany had asked for the doll instead. "Brittany, we don't know if it's all right with Kimmy's and Melanie's mommies," she hedged.

"I'm sure it'll be fine," Caleb assured her. "Kimmy is my younger sister Sallie's kid, and Melanie belongs to my brother Cody and his wife, Donna Jean. The more the merrier, as far as they're concerned. They're real laid-back."

Cheyenne was not reassured. Suppose laid-back meant permitting the children to run loose and unsupervised? The Strongs lived so close to the river, so close to the railroad tracks. She tried to remember if she'd heard of any deaths by drowning or being hit by a train among the Strongs. She did recall a neighborhood picnic that summer when David Beckworth, the town's pediatrician, had regaled everyone present with the tale of a Strong toddler who had climbed out of an open window and fallen two stories, landing on one of the family pets.

"The kid had a few bruises, the dog had a few bruises, but neither were seriously hurt," Beckworth had joked. "The Strongs have nine lives, just like their cats. Even their dogs do." Everyone at the party had laughed appreciatively, then they had all berated the Strongs in absentia for neglectful parenting. After all, no one in the Silver Creek neighborhood had ever had a child who'd fallen out a window!

"Cheyenne," Joni Lynn said quietly, "you don't have to be afraid of Brittany going to either Aunt Sallie's or Aunt Donna's. They take good care of their kids."

Cheyenne colored painfully. Having lived with her for a whole year, Joni Lynn had come to know her well. Very well. She'd practically read her mind, and Cheyenne was sorry and ashamed that it had been filled with Strong apprehensions. She glanced hesitantly at Caleb.

He stared back at her, his eyes hard. He was annoyed with himself for forgetting, even for an instant, the social chasm that stretched between them. He had his own insights into Cheyenne's hesitancy: She didn't consider his nieces and their homes good enough for the offspring of a Whitney.

The attraction he felt for her seemed like a betrayal to his family, to his own sense of self. A deep anger stirred within him.

It was Cheyenne's turn at mind reading. Caleb, she knew, was categorizing her with the likes of Dawn Bentley and Lily Thurman and all the others. She suddenly felt desperate to show him that he was wrong.

"I've never let Brittany or Jeffrey go to any child's house unless I've met the parents first," she said quickly, and looked to Joni Lynn for confirmation.

"That's right," Joni Lynn said, nodding. "It's a sensible policy, Uncle Caleb."

He said nothing, nothing at all. He'd already tried her and found her guilty, Cheyenne thought miserably.

"Am I playing with Kimmy and Melanie?" Brittany asked.

"I'll call and ask their mothers if they're allowed to come here and play tomorrow after school," Cheyenne said. She was ostensibly talking to Brittany, but her eyes appealed to Caleb.

He didn't glance her way.

"I want to go to Kimmy's," Brittany persisted, which was rare for her. Unlike her brother, she usually accepted her mother's word without question or challenge. "Kimmy has a hundred Barbies and I only have five. I want to play with a hundred Barbies."

"Brittany, that's an exaggeration," Cheyenne said. "Kimmy doesn't have a hundred Barbie dolls."

"Actually, she does," Joni Lynn said. "I helped her count them. She has a hundred and two. Kimmy is an only child, and Aunt Sallie is a doll freak," she added, by way of explanation.

"Please, can I go, Mommy?" Brittany asked, dazzled by the prospect.

"Brittany, honey, I think you'd better drop it," Caleb said in a voice that brooked no argument. "Your mother doesn't want you to go and that's that."

Brittany sighed, scowled, then sighed again with resignation.

Jeffrey, growing bored, jumped down from his chair. "I want my dessert," he announced.

Normally, Cheyenne would have insisted that he remain seated until everyone at the table had finished eating. That night, though, she was grateful for the diversion. "Carry your plate into the kitchen first, Jeffrey," she said.

"And don't give Peppy any chicken bones, no matter how much he begs," Joni Lynn reminded him. "They're not good for him."

Urgently needing to escape from Caleb and the condemnation she felt radiating from him, Cheyenne turned to the kitchen. "Peppy can be very persuasive. I'd better go watch him."

She hurried out of the dining room. Brittany followed her a moment later, her plate in hand. As usual, she hadn't finished the small portions Cheyenne had given her.

"I'm done!" the little girl sang out. Brittany never ate much, but it always concerned Cheyenne.

"Darling, you hardly touched your peas. And you left almost half your chicken and—"

"I'm stuffed, Mommy." Brittany didn't care for a postmortem of her meal and quickly raced out of the kitchen.

Peppy, honing on Brittany's plate as if by radar, put his front paws on the counter and snatched the half-eaten piece of chicken. Holding the contraband morsel in his teeth, he dashed between Joni Lynn and Caleb, who were coming into the kitchen with their empty plates.

"Oh, no!" Joni Lynn cried. "I'll get it from him." She shoved her plate into Caleb's hands and ran after the dog, who was circling the dining room table with the piece of chicken dangling from his mouth. Brittany and Jeffrey were already chasing after him.

"The farcical chase scene. Another TV sitcom staple,"

Caleb said, watching the three of them and the dog race around the table. He set his and Joni Lynn's plates down. "Thanks for dinner," he added to Cheyenne. "I'm leaving now, but before I go I'd like to talk to you about Joni Lynn's expenses."

"You're leaving now?" Cheyenne felt her heart sink like a stone. "But you haven't had dessert," she protested weakly.

"I'll pass. About Joni Lynn . . . I heard you've been shouldering all of her living expenses and—"

"I know you're angry with me," she blurted out. She wasn't as shocked by her outburst this time. She was beginning to get used to speaking her mind around Caleb Strong.

"I'm not angry," he said in a tight, clipped voice that completely belied his words. "I'm in a hurry to leave, and I want to discuss Joni Lynn's expenses—"

"Caleb, I wasn't casting aspersions upon your family by not immediately agreeing to let Brittany play at Kimmy's house. It's just that I'm uneasy about letting the children go anywhere when I haven't—"

This time he cut her off. "So you said. And Joni Lynn backed you up, which is exactly what I would've expected from her. She's very loyal to you. There is no way she could let herself believe that you share this town's aversion to anything Strong."

"But I don't!"

He rolled his eyes heavenward in sarcastic dismissal of her claim. "As I've been trying to say, I know that you've been paying all Joni Lynn's living expenses since she moved in here. My sister Crystal told me that she hasn't contributed a cent to the kid's support. I don't think that's fair, and I want to reimburse you."

He reached into his pocket and pulled out that eye-popping money roll. "Here." He peeled off several one-hundred-dollar bills. "From now on, I'll be sending you money for her support monthly."

She backed away from him, from the bills. "I can't

take your money. When I invited Joni Lynn to move in, I didn't expect to be monetarily compensated for it."

"'Monetarily compensated.' 'Casting aspersions.'" He gave a short, mocking laugh. "You sound exactly like the stiff, prissy English teacher you are." He took a step closer, and she instinctively retreated. "What's the matter, lady? Isn't my money good enough for a stuck-up small-town princess like you?"

It was just too much. Cheyenne, long noted for her equable disposition and placid temperament, abandoned both as the tension that had been building inside her exploded into rage.

"Do you know what you are, *Mr. Strong*? You're a reverse snob." She quivered with outrage. "You don't want to believe that I might be different from the Bentleys and the Thurmans and the Mayfields and everybody else. You enjoy clinging to your preconceived and prejudged stereotypes just as much as they do."

Her breasts heaved as she fairly panted with anger and frustration. "You're every bit as blind and obstinate as they are."

Caleb's gaze was riveted to her breasts. The night before he had felt their fullness. They had filled his hands, soft and firm and rounded. The sensual memory hit him with the force of a speeding freight train, leaving him momentarily winded. And furious at his own weakness. Defensively, he turned the fury on her.

"Now she's a psychoanalyst," he taunted. "The princess is a lady of so many talents."

The insolence in his tone further inflamed her. "You just proved my point. Princess. Lady." She flung the words at him. "You relish branding me, just like people in this town have delighted in pinning nasty labels on you and your kin. You claim to hate the prejudice and the snobbery in Whitneyville, but you're just as steeped in it. You condemn people like the Bentleys and the Thurmans, but you're the flip side of the same coin."

"Are you finished?"

Caleb's show of cool indifference demanded every ounce of his formidable willpower, for the anger raging inside him was near flash point. He was incensed by her and her accusations. She'd used her English teacher semantics to present her absurd, faulty logic. If her offensive premise made an ominous bit of sense, it was because she was verbally clever, he assured himself, not because it was even slightly true.

"Yes, I'm finished," she said. "You've shut yourself behind a self-righteous, unresponsive wall, and I know how useless it is to try to reason with that kind of determined opposition. I faced the same concrete mind-set from certain people in this town when Joni Lynn came to live here. You're just the reverse side of the mirror."

"Flip side of the coin. Reverse side of the mirror. The English teacher also speaks in clichéd metaphors." He paced to the kitchen door and back. It was impossible to stand still when his body was vibrating with tension. "Well, I'll give it to you straight, lady. Stop comparing me to the arrogant, supercilious snobs in this pretentious town. I'm nothing like them, not in any way!"

She tilted her chin up defiantly. "'There is none so blind as he who will not see,'" she quoted.

"You just don't know when to quit, do you, baby?" he said raspily. "You keep on pushing and pushing . . . until it's too late."

Cheyenne heard the raw fury in his voice and saw it in his eyes, in the rigidity of his powerful body. She mentally likened her predicament to someone who had just pulled the tail of a sleeping tiger, only to discover the ferocious beast was awake—and bent on seeking revenge.

Five

Perhaps it was the wild activity in the adjacent dining room that inspired her response, or perhaps it was Caleb's own restless pacing. Whatever, Cheyenne felt the need for some kind of action herself. She took off, heading out the kitchen door to the back porch.

She was halfway down the porch stairs when Caleb caught her around the waist with one arm and swung her back up the stairs, handling her as easily as that metaphorical tiger might maneuver its hapless prey.

"Stop manhandling me!" she demanded when her feet touched ground again on the porch. She spoke with far more bravado than she was feeling. With Caleb's arm wrapped around her like a steel band, she could hardly breathe.

"Oh, baby, what a lead-in." He laughed roughly, and he didn't loosen his grip. "Now I get to make the obvious comeback—that you've been begging for a man to handle you."

"And you accused me of talking in clichés! Your so-called comeback is as worn and trite a one as I've ever heard. Not to mention completely untrue."

He walked her backward until they reached the porch wall. "Honey, when a woman runs from a man the way you just did, it's the equivalent of an engraved invitation for him to go after her and catch her."

She forced herself to meet his eyes. "It could also mean that she can't stand to be around him. That she's had enough of his stubborn, pigheaded, opinionated—" She had to pause, both to breathe and to search her mind for more derogatory adjectives.

He pushed her against the wall and pinned her there, between it and his body. As he towered over her, she was struck again by how big and strong and virile he was. Her gaze fixed on his face. The fire in his eyes was hot enough to burn, and she felt its molten effects deep within her. The anger that had been sustaining her began to melt, leaving her dangerously weak and soft.

Bracing one hand near her head, he leaned into her, his body heavy and hard against hers. "Admit it. This is what you *planned* to have happen when you ran out here."

His head lowered to hers until his mouth was a tantalizing inch above her lips. It would be so easy, she thought, to close her eyes and relax against his solid, masculine strength. She ached for the feel of his mouth on hers. She'd been aching for it since he'd kissed her the night before, and she'd been wanting more, wanting him again, all last night and through the day. But to let him know that, to give in to him after the high-handed way he'd treated her . . .

Her pride rebelled at the notion. "I'll admit to no such thing!" She managed to wedge her hands between them and push against his chest. She couldn't budge him, but it didn't stop her from trying.

"You've been offensive and insulting," she exclaimed, "and now you expect me to give in to your caveman tactics. Well, I won't. My children and your niece and the dog are running around the house, and I'm angry with you, and the last thing I had in mind

was any sort of—of romantic encounter when I came
out here!"

"Romantic encounter? Is that what you call it?" In
spite of his great efforts to hold on to it, Caleb's anger
was fading. He felt more like smiling than scowling.
He found her indignation and her determination to
stand up to him both amusing and appealing. She
was small and undaunted, feisty and ladylike, and
the combination was irresistible.

He had planned to grind his mouth into hers in an
insulting, punishing kiss, then walk away in scorn-
ful dismissal. Instead, he brushed his lips lightly,
seductively, across hers, wooing her.

Cheyenne's puny defenses crumbled under his sensual coaxing. A small sigh escaped from her, and she
slid her arms around his neck. It seemed inevitable,
fated, that they come together again, in passion and
urgency. Hot pleasure rippled through her as his lips
took hers in a deep, demanding kiss.

Her mouth opened under his, welcoming the slow
thrust of his tongue as it sank into her moist heat,
probing and rubbing with bold intimacy. They kissed
wildly, ravenously, oblivious to time, place, and cir-
cumstance.

A radiant heat swept through Cheyenne. She felt
her breasts swell and squirmed against him, pressing herself to the solid wall of his chest. Her nipples
were tight and almost painfully sensitive, and she
couldn't stop herself from rubbing them against him.
It wasn't enough. She wanted to bare herself to him,
to let him touch her there . . . with his fingers . . .
with his mouth.

Her head was spinning. She'd never had such
thoughts before about anyone except Evan, and even
with him, sexual excitement had soon died. It was
astonishing to think that her mind had harbored
these secret ideas and desires—and that Caleb
Strong had unleashed them.

Their legs were intimately entwined, and when he
rocked against her, she was acutely aware of his

arousal, hard and thick against her. She was just as excruciatingly aware of her own aching emptiness, of the ever-growing need to be filled with him, by him.

Caleb stroked his hands over her possessively, touching as much of her as he could. They kissed and kissed, long, slow, deep kisses that grew more ardent, more passionate, more intimate. At last he tore his mouth from hers and pressed it against the slender curve of her neck. He nipped at the sensitive skin, then soothed it with his tongue. She shivered and clung to him.

"I'm hungry for you," he growled huskily. "I'm burning for you. I was awake most of last night, tossing and turning and pacing because I wanted you so badly, I was half crazy with it."

His raw confession thrilled her. She'd never thought she was capable of inspiring passion or need in a man. She had certainly failed to do so with Evan. But here was Caleb Strong, a man of experience, a man well acquainted with lust, telling her how much he wanted her.

She drew back her head a little and gazed up at him, her eyes unfocused with passion. "Really?" she whispered. "You're not just saying that?"

"I don't lie about what I want and need from a woman," he murmured, his voice deep and rough. "And I want it all from you, baby." He claimed her mouth once more in a rapacious, wanton kiss.

This time when he lifted his lips from hers, she had to hang on to him. Her legs were so shaky and weak, they couldn't support her, but her arms clasped him with all her strength. She even dared to touch her mouth to the hard, tanned column of his neck. How was it possible, she wondered, to feel so languorous yet so vitally energized at the same time?

"Tonight," he whispered against her ear. His tongue traced the delicate outer shell, and sensual shivers tingled through her. "I'll come over after the kids are asleep."

It took a moment for his words to penetrate the

drowsy mists of passion that enshrouded her mind, but then the full implication dawned. If Caleb Strong came over after the children were asleep, it wouldn't be to walk Peppy or to sit on the front porch and chat as they sipped lemonade. She gulped. "You want to—to go to bed with me?"

"Oh, yeah, baby." He laughed huskily. "I definitely want to go to bed with you." He pulled her back to kiss her again.

Cheyenne ducked her head, and his lips grazed her cheek instead of capturing her mouth. She was being propositioned for the first time in her life! And the speed with which they'd gone from renewing an old acquaintance to kissing to—to sleeping together?—was dizzying.

"Caleb Strong is fast."

A giggling voice from the past leaped into her consciousness. Suddenly she could see herself as a fourteen-year-old freshman in the girls' bathroom at Whitneyville High. She was nervously combing her hair at the mirror while slutty Penny Sherwood and her bad-girl group of friends were illicitly smoking in the largest stall and swapping confidences.

"Tell us about that hickey on your belly, Penny," another girl said, and they all giggled. Cheyenne had fled, her cheeks burning.

Her cheeks were burning now. Caleb Strong was still fast! And he wanted to cast her in the Penny Sherwood role.

"On second thought, why wait till tonight?" He took her hand in his and started toward the door. "Let's go now. Tell Joni Lynn to look after the kids, and I'll take you over to the Magic Carpet."

"The Magic Carpet Motel?" Cheyenne echoed, aghast.

She visualized the place, a seedy relic from the days before the interstate highway had diverted tourists from the old two-lane local roads. Now the motel catered only to the occasional traveler, although it was said to do a brisk business in hourly rentals.

Caleb was too intent on his destination to notice her horrified expression. "It's out on Route Six on the way to Smithboro," he said offhandedly. The thought of Cheyenne lying naked and willing under him took his breath away. His body throbbed with urgency, and he hustled her into the kitchen.

Cheyenne's gaze swept over her homey green-and-yellow kitchen, with her collection of ceramic cookie jars and the children's papers tacked to the refrigerator with colorful magnets. It was the kitchen of a respectable lady, a mother and a teacher, hardly the sort of woman who ran off to the Magic Carpet Motel with a man she'd known two days, give or take fourteen years.

She grabbed the side of the counter and held on with one hand while jerking her other hand away from his. "I know where the Magic Carpet Motel is," she spluttered. "But I can't believe you actually think I'd go there! Who do you think I am? Penny Sherwood?"

Caleb's eyes slowly became less glazed as he focused on her, clinging to the counter, her expression outraged. "What?" he asked, still feeling dazed. He couldn't remember the last time he'd been aroused so quickly, so wildly. Proper, highborn Cheyenne Whitney turned him on as he'd never been turned on before. The revelation had him reeling.

"Who?" he asked blankly.

"Penny Sherwood!" Cheyenne snapped. "Your high school girlfriend. I certainly remember her, even if *you* don't!"

"I had lots of girlfriends in high school," he snapped back. "And that was a long time ago."

"Let me refresh your memory, then. According to Whitneyville legend, Penny Sherwood is the one who broke into the high school building with you on Halloween night, and then the two of you—"

"Oh. Now I remember. *That* Penny Sherwood." The corners of his mouth tilted into a sexy grin. "Wonder where she is and what she's doing these days?"

"Well, if she's smart, these days she's charging by the hour instead of giving it away for free like she used to!"

Cheyenne stiffened with shock as her words seemed to echo in the quiet kitchen. If she hadn't heard herself say it, she wouldn't have believed herself capable of such a blunt, unladylike remark. Gracious, it sounded like something Penny Sherwood herself might say!

Caleb burst into laughter. Spending time with Cheyenne was like riding a triple-loop roller coaster, he decided. His emotions had raced from anger to passion to laughter with breathless rapidity. He felt as off balance as she looked, and he knew he should be beating a path to the front door because she disturbed him as no other woman ever had. But as he thought of her acerbic slam at that youthful sexual adventuress, Penny Sherwood, he only laughed harder.

"It's not funny!" she exclaimed. "I've never said anything so dreadful in my life. I—I apologize."

"Why? It was an honest observation. And Penny isn't around to hear anyway. She's probably plying her . . . er, wares in—"

"Will you hush?" Cheyenne interrupted frantically. "I don't want to discuss it—her—anymore."

She rushed from the kitchen into the dining room, which was empty and silent. The sound of the children's laughter drew her to the front door. They were all out in the yard. Jeffrey was sitting on Peppy, who lay sprawled on the grass, while Joni Lynn pried the chicken from the dog's mouth. Ever good-natured, Peppy didn't snap or bite or even fight, but cheerfully surrendered his catch.

Caleb came to stand beside Cheyenne. "It's time for me to leave." He wondered if she would protest, perhaps insist that he stay for dessert. It worried him that he wanted her to.

She didn't. Cheyenne didn't trust herself even to glance at him. She'd already behaved like a candidate for the Magic Carpet Motel. She was not about to compound her mistake in any way. "Thank you again," she said stiltedly, "for the gifts you bought Jeffrey and Brittany this afternoon." Her gaze remained fixed on the children, who were now throwing sticks for Peppy to retrieve.

She felt Caleb's fingers brush hers, and he shoved something stiff and starchy into her hand. Even before she'd ascertained it was money, he said crisply. "You're going to take it and keep it. You can't afford to support another person and don't try to pretend you don't need money."

"What do you mean?" she demanded. She considered opening her hand and letting the bills fall to the ground, but resisted the impulse. The way things were going, Peppy would probably spot them and retrieve them. Or eat them.

"I mean," he said bluntly, "that you're not a rich widow like people in this town think you are, not by a long shot. You don't work just to keep busy or to get out of the house. You work because you have bills to pay and a family to support."

He was right, of course, but it rankled her to hear him state the facts. Discussing someone's financial status simply was *not* done. It might be whispered about behind one's back, but to be confronted with it? Never! "And how did you happen to draw your particular conclusion?" she asked stiffly.

"It was easy. I took a good look around this place. The house needs to be painted, and I'll wager that the roof needs to be replaced just as badly. Your furniture is beyond what passes for shabby genteel. It's plain worn-out, and that goes for the rugs too. The appliances in the kitchen are at least forty years old and—"

"I'm sorry my house doesn't meet your high standards," she interjected icily. That he was absolutely right on all points made it all the more unbearable. After paying their usual monthly expenses, she never had enough money to cover big projects like having the house repainted or the roof reshingled. She'd already sold the few good pieces of antique furniture to make ends meet. The ancient sofa and chairs in the living room and the old kitchen appliances were nobody's idea of antiques. Junk for the local dump was closer to the mark.

"Aren't you going to make some comment about how anything worn-out and owned by a Whitney is still worth more than anything brand-new that's owned by a lowly Strong?" he asked.

"I'm not the one dishing out the insults here, you are," she said. "First about me personally, then about my house."

"Wait a minute. When did I insult you personally?"

"Have you already forgotten your invitation to the Magic Carpet Motel? I certainly haven't."

He scowled. "You're insulted because I wanted to make love with you?"

She whirled to face him. "Make love? A one-night stand at a sleazy motel has nothing to do with love and everything to do with—with cheap sex. Of course, I'm insulted that you think I'm a tramp, someone to be rushed off to a squalid place like the Magic Carpet!"

"What I thought was that you're a passionate woman who wanted me as much as I wanted you. That doesn't make you a tramp in my eyes."

"Is that supposed to make me feel better? Well, it doesn't! You probably didn't think Penny Sherwood was a tramp either. You even took her to the Junior-Senior Winter Carnival Dance, one of the biggest social events of the school year."

He frowned in puzzlement. "What?"

"I saw you there together. I was one of the ten freshmen girls chosen to dress up as elves and serve refreshments at the dance that year. Penny Sherwood shocked the chaperons by showing up in a tight, slinky red dress that was backless and cut indecently low in front, and the principal told you both to leave. But before you did, you managed to spike the raspberry sherbet punch with vodka!"

"Oh. *That* dance." He heaved an exasperated sigh. "How do you remember all this junk?" His gaze turned speculative. "And why?"

Cheyenne felt her cheeks flush. His questions were unanswerable. Why did she seem to remember every detail about Caleb Strong? Why did she collect those long-ago memories, most of which didn't even directly involve her?

"You must lead an intolerably dull life if you have to get your kicks by dredging up my past," he said, taunting her.

"I don't!"

"Well," he went on idly, "I offered you a chance to break out of your straightjacket existence tonight, but you prefer vicarious thrills, don't you, Miss Cheyenne? You'd rather fantasize about me and Penny Sherwood than risk experiencing the real thing with me."

He shrugged and ambled out onto the front porch. "It's your loss, honey," he called softly over his shoulder. "Even your steamiest fantasies couldn't match the reality I'd show you."

Cheyenne's whole body was one hot blush. She was alternately humiliated and titillated as his parting shot echoed in her ears. Then she decided she was enraged and had every right to be. *He* had insulted *her*, then somehow turned things around so that *she* was the one on the defensive. She should have ordered him to leave, but he had chosen to walk out first. His departure was yet another insult to her pride.

She watched as he called good-bye to Joni Lynn, Brittany, and Jeffrey. Her gaze never wavered from him as he straddled his motorcycle and sped off without so much as a wave or backward glance.

She didn't realize she was clenching her hands tightly into fists until her fingers began to ache. Slowly, she uncurled them and found herself staring at the crisp, new bills Caleb had given her. It seemed natural to count them and she did, then stared in shock when she had finished.

Ten. There were ten one-hundred-dollar bills in her hand. He had given her a thousand dollars for Joni Lynn's past expenses and had promised to send more. She thought of his spending spree at Bentley's earlier that afternoon. Where was he getting all this money? And why did he carry it around with him? One did not flash cash in Whitneyville, one used checks or credit. Perhaps he found it inopportune to use either. Checks and credit slips left a paper trail. Was there some reason why he preferred the anonymity of cash? Some sinister, ominous reason?

So many questions were swirling around in her head, all of them about Caleb Strong. Images of him, both past and present, seemed to be imprinted indelibly in her mind. She couldn't think of anything or anyone else.

She made it through the rest of the evening on automatic pilot, and fortunately, neither Brittany, Jeffrey, nor Joni Lynn seemed to notice her preoccupation.

When she took Peppy for his late-night walk, she was unhappily aware of how very much she wished to hear the roar of a big black motorcycle on Silver Creek Road. *She wanted to be with Caleb Strong!* It was shattering, unthinkable. But it was true. He was gone, and she missed him already.

Cheyenne hadn't cried herself to sleep in years, not since that terrible night when she'd received the phone call from one of Evan's college fraternity brothers in Atlanta, informing her of her husband's fatal car accident while visiting his girlfriend there in the city. Caleb's departure from her life hardly ranked with that event, but try as she might, she couldn't hold back the tears that streamed from her eyes.

Eventually, drained and exhausted, she fell into a restless, troubled sleep.

Six

Cheyenne was in her kitchen the next afternoon, readying a meat loaf for the oven, when the back door opened and Tricia Vance Harper, her best friend since kindergarten, and Tricia's six-year-old daughter Mollie walked in. Tricia never bothered to knock or use the front door. She lived a block away and cut through a back alley to Cheyenne's kitchen door.

"Where's Brittany?" Mollie demanded. "My grandma bought me two new dolls, and I want to show her. They're ones she doesn't have," the little girl added smugly.

Cheyenne suppressed a sigh. Unlike herself and Tricia, Brittany and Mollie did not seem destined to follow the path of lifelong friendship. At six, the age when Cheyenne and Tricia had been inseparable, always wanting to dress alike and pretend to be twin sisters, Brittany and Mollie simply did not like each other.

"Brittany is upstairs playing with Jeffrey," Cheyenne said, determinedly pasting a smile on her face. The peace in the house would soon come to an end, for Mollie and Jeffrey *actively* disliked each other.

"Ross has his Rotary Club dinner meeting tonight," Tricia said as Mollie skipped off, "and I wondered if you and the kids want to have dinner at the White Horse Inn with Mollie and me."

"Oh, I'd like to, but I've already made dinner." That was Cheyenne's usual reply to Tricia's monthly Rotary Club night invitations. Though the White Horse Inn had an informal, family-type dining room, it was still too high-priced for her careful budget.

Tricia stared critically at the baking pan. "That's dinner? What in heaven's name is it?"

"Ribbon meat loaf. It has slices of American cheese in the middle, and they melt to look like a ribbon running through." Cheyenne slid the pan into the oven.

"Oh, *puh-leese!*" Tricia made a terrible face. "If I tried to give that to Ross and Mollie, they'd throw it back at me. Come on, Cheyenne, we haven't been out together in ages. Deep-six the ribbon loaf and come with us."

Cheyenne began to peel and slice a bunch of carrots. "I really can't, Trish. Joni Lynn gets home from her job at the ice-cream shop at quarter to six, and she'll—"

"Ah, yes, Joni Lynn, your goodwill project. Your little foster sister." Tricia plopped down onto one of the kitchen chairs. "According to Dawn Bentley, you've become a champion for the rest of the Strongs as well."

"Dawn Bentley?" Cheyenne's hands stilled. "What did she say?"

"That yesterday afternoon a whole mob of Strong brats pushed their way into the store and just about wrecked it, and when she tried to calm them down, you became totally irrational and started yelling at her."

"So that's the way she's attempting to justify her behavior?" Cheyenne tossed down the carrot peeler and turned to face her friend. "It didn't happen that way, Tricia. Dawn was the irrational one doing the yelling. She behaved abominably and she knows it."

"Cheyenne, there's more." Tricia leaned forward in her chair. "Dawn also claims that Caleb Strong was there with a big wad of drug money that she didn't want spent in her store. When she tried to stop him, you leaped to his defense, insulted her, then allowed him to buy presents for Brittany and Jeffrey with his quote—filthy drug dollars—unquote."

"Caleb Strong is not a drug dealer!" Cheyenne exclaimed.

"The word around town is that he carries a roll of cash that could choke a horse. Typical drug dealer behavior."

"Tricia, how would you know? You've never seen a drug dealer in your life."

"Well, every drug dealer in every movie and television show I've ever seen carries a lot of cash," Tricia retorted. "And you have to admit, it does seem suspicious. Where else would a Strong get that kind of money? And since when are you so chummy with Caleb Strong that you and your kids go shopping with him?"

"We weren't shopping with him," Cheyenne said in a strangled voice as she grabbed the peeler. She could feel heat sweeping from the tip of her toes to her forehead and quickly turned around, attacking the carrots, her hands shaking. "We happened to run into him and we talked to him. He is Joni Lynn's uncle, you know."

"Befriending sweet little Joni Lynn is one thing, Cheyenne. Caleb Strong is an entirely different matter. Not even being a Whitney could salvage your reputation if—heaven forbid—you were linked with *him*!"

Cheyenne sighed. "I had enough lectures from my parents when I was growing up about the responsibilities of living up to the Whitney name, Trish. I don't need another one from you at this late date."

"Is that how I sounded?" Tricia looked sheepish. "Sorry. Don't be mad at me, Cheyenne."

She smiled. "I'm not."

"Great! Then you'll come to dinner next Friday? Ross's sister and her husband will be visiting from Charleston, and we're having a small party for them."

"Oh, Trish, I really can't. I—"

"Stop! I know all your excuses by heart. Joni Lynn works late on Fridays so you have to find a sitter, which is almost impossible because all the kids in town go to the high school football games. And you're tired on Friday nights from working all week long and you just like to stay in and relax."

Cheyenne smiled wryly. "I'm glad you understand, Tricia."

"Oh, I do. But this time I'm not taking no for an answer. I've already asked Darcey Jo Simmons to baby-sit for Brittany and Jeffrey, and she agreed. She's twelve now and can certainly handle the job. You can relax at my house, Cheyenne. We're just having some old friends over to dinner—Polly and Graham Maitland, the Russells, the Smiths. You know them all very well."

"Yes, but . . ."

"Evan has been dead for four and a half years, Cheyenne," Tricia said gently. "I know it's difficult, but you really have to start getting out more often. Say you'll come."

There was really no reasonable excuse not to, Cheyenne admitted glumly to herself. Tricia had successfully demolished all her tried-and-true reasons, including her most effective one, that of her as the grieving widow. Stifling a groan, she agreed to go.

"Oh, I almost forgot to mention that Graham's brother Ben will be there," Tricia said brightly. "He's newly divorced and just moved back to town from Savannah. He'll be working in the Whitneyville Bank as a loan officer. You remember Ben, don't you? He played Curley in the high school music club's production of *Oklahoma* the year he was a senior and we were freshmen. Remember how cute he was?"

Cheyenne remembered, but she couldn't feign enthusiasm about their enforced pairing at Tricia's party. For the first time ever, she welcomed the sound of Jeffrey's roar of fury. It was followed immediately by a high-pitched shriek of outrage. "I'd better check on the kids," she said quickly.

"I'll go with you," Tricia said, and the unmistakable sounds of quarreling children precluded any more reminiscences or party plans.

"Uncle Caleb is leaving tonight," Joni Lynn said with a regretful sigh as she and Cheyenne washed the dinner dishes. "He stopped by the ice-cream shop this afternoon to say good-bye to me."

Cheyenne let the bowl she was washing slip back into the soapy water. "Did he say when he would be coming back?" she heard herself ask.

Her stomach was churning, and it took great effort to keep her voice steady. She knew she was overreacting to a piece of news that shouldn't concern her in the least. She should be glad he was going so she could resume her tranquil existence.

"No, he never says. Uncle Caleb comes and goes." Joni Lynn shrugged. "I think he came this time because my mom has been having more trouble with my little brother. He's been skipping school again and getting into fights whenever he does go."

"And your mother depends on your Uncle Caleb for advice?" Cheyenne asked, a little shocked at how hungry she was for information about him.

Joni Lynn nodded. "Everybody in the family does. My great-uncle Ralph calls Uncle Caleb 'The Chief.' He gives advice and support and money. Oh, and lectures too," she added, grinning.

Money. There it was again. Cheyenne was so consumed by the mystery of Caleb Strong's unexplained source of income, she broke every rule of etiquette and asked with unabashed curiosity, "Exactly what does your uncle Caleb do, Joni Lynn?"

The girl shifted uncomfortably. "Well, I—I'm not exactly sure."

Cheyenne knew at once she wasn't telling the truth. "I didn't mean to pry, Joni Lynn," she said, and felt her face flame at the blatant lie. She'd been prying for all she was worth!

"Oh, Cheyenne, I feel awful keeping anything from you, but I'm not supposed to tell what Uncle Caleb does or who he works for. He says it's a secret that only the Strongs are allowed to know. I just can't tell you. I'm sorry!"

"It's all right." Cheyenne forced a smile. "I had no business asking anyway." A secret only for the Strongs to know? she repeated silently, and felt an ominous foreboding. Tricia's accusation was echoing in her ears.

"I understand why Uncle Caleb feels the way he does," Joni Lynn went on, her eyes troubled. "But I don't agree with the secrecy. I mean, it's not illegal for a Strong to be successful, although Uncle Caleb says in this town it may as well be."

"But he—What he does isn't illegal, is it?" Cheyenne was ashamed of the question and of herself for asking it, but she simply couldn't *not* ask.

"No, of course not!" Joni Lynn exclaimed, as if shocked by the very idea. "Not my uncle Caleb!"

The relief that ripped through Cheyenne was abruptly replaced by irritation. This was maddening! Caleb Strong's penchant for secrecy was totally different from her open and straightforward relationship with Joni Lynn. "Are you allowed to tell where your uncle lives?" she asked, a shade caustically.

"I don't see why not. He lives in Mobile, Alabama." Joni Lynn was eager to volunteer this bit of unclassified information. "But he does a lot of traveling. He says he has lots of homes away from home. We tease him that his home away from home in Whitneyville is the Magic Carpet Motel."

A plate fell from Cheyenne's suddenly nerveless

fingers. It crashed to the floor, breaking on impact. "How clumsy of me!" she said shakily, stooping to pick up the pieces. "You were saying that your uncle frequents the . . . er, Magic Carpet Motel?"

"He stays there every time he comes to Whitneyville because he likes his privacy and doesn't want to inconvenience the family by anyone having to put him up. The Magic Carpet has kind of a bad reputation, but Uncle Caleb says the rooms are big and clean and cheap and perfectly adequate." Joni Lynn chuckled. "He calls staying there cost containment. He's really big on that."

Cheyenne was wondering why the fact that Caleb had been a registered guest at the motel somehow made his suggestion to take her there less . . . scandalous. Taking her to *his* room instead of *a* room struck her as less of an insult and more of an invitation. After all, it was hardly an insult to be invited to someone's home, and if the Magic Carpet was his "home away from home," then . . .

"You're a passionate woman who wanted me as much as I wanted you. That doesn't make you a tramp in my eyes." As his words replayed in her head, she found herself believing him.

And that alarmed her! Her powers of rationalization were downright frightening when it came to justifying Caleb's words and deeds. It was definitely all for the best that he was leaving town. Why, she was on the verge of talking herself in to believing that a clandestine tryst with him at the Magic Carpet Motel wasn't so very sordid after all. The man was dangerous, a threat to her peace of mind, her virtue, and her reputation.

So why couldn't her formidable rationalizing powers convince her she was happy he was gone?

The unpretentious building housing Dix-Mart corporate headquarters was located in suburban Mobile, away from the congestion and traffic of the city. Caleb pulled the silver-gray Buick, his company car, into his reserved parking space, greeted the attendant with a wave, and entered the building. He owned and drove a fire-engine-red Corvette, his one and only status symbol, off the job—though not when he was in Whitneyville, of course. There, he used the big black Harley he kept at his brother's place to travel around town in character, while the Corvette was lodged in a garage in the neighboring town of Smithboro.

Inside the office building, he spoke to everyone and they all greeted him. His dark blue suit was impeccably tailored, his white shirt custom-made, his striped tie pure silk. He was the quintessential image of the young, successful executive and far, far removed from the rebel role he played in Whitneyville.

He was smiling as he walked into his office. Coming back here, to the Dix-Mart Building in Mobile, was truly like coming home. The plaque on his office door read C. W. Strong, but didn't carry his title, executive vice-president. It didn't have to. Everybody in the company knew him and his position. As he entered the wide, roomy office, he felt the sense of pride and satisfaction he always experienced there. Before sitting down at his massive desk, he glanced out the wall of windows at the pastoral countryside. Best view in the whole building, he thought smugly.

A few minutes later, Preston Ralburn, company president and son-in-law of Mack Dixon, Dix-Mart's founder and chairman of the board, dropped in.

"So we finally won in Whitneyville," Ralburn said, clasping Caleb's hand in a firm shake. "Hard to believe their chamber of commerce kept us tied up in court for four years! That's the longest fight we've had."

"They're tenacious in Whitneyville," Caleb said with a grim smile. "Any kind of change goes against the grain—which is why our store is going to be a smashing success there. Downtown Whitneyville is like stepping into the past. A bad past. Service is terrible, merchandise is poorly displayed. Forget marketing. I don't think Whitneyville is aware of the concept. And the attitude of the store owners is 'we're doing you a big favor by letting you spend your money here.' I predict that within a month of our opening, the pretentious, pathetic stores of Whitneyville will start collapsing like the proverbial house of cards."

Ralburn beamed. "And Dix-Mart will have scored another big hit with another Discount City. No one can pinpoint a location for a Dix-Mart like you can, Caleb. Your instincts are positively uncanny. Whitneyville will make the five hundred and fifth successful store location for you. And all of those stores are our biggest money-makers."

Caleb shrugged. "It's research, not instinct, Ral."

"If it were purely research, then all the stores would be earning out the same as yours. Don't try to be modest, Caleb. Face facts—you're infallible."

The two men laughed good-naturedly. "Karen wants you to come out to the house for dinner tomorrow," Ralburn added as he was leaving. "Mack will be there too. Around seven?"

"Sounds good."

"And be forewarned, Karen has invited a certain Lindsey Carroll as well. Lindsey's mother is an old school chum of Karen's. Need I say more?"

"Help!" Caleb groaned. "Not another of Karen's matchmaking attempts!"

"Karen is determined to see you settled and happily married," Ralburn said with a chuckle. "She won't quit until you are. As long as you remain one of Mobile's most eligible bachelors, Karen is going to keep serving up delicious young dishes. And I'm not talking about home cooking." Laughing at his own atrocious pun, Ralburn left the office.

One of Mobile's most eligible bachelors. Caleb shook his head. It was always a stunning reversal in perception to come back to Mobile from Whitneyville. In his old hometown, he was an outcast and a misfit, his name synonymous with loser. In his new hometown, he was a rising star in a phenomenally successful billion-dollar corporation, and was considered a "catch." In Mobile, Karen Dixon Ralburn, daughter of Dix-Mart's founder, wife of the company president, and member of one of the city's most influential families, was a close friend. She was forever inviting him to dinner and trying to fix him up with "a nice young lady of quality." In Whitneyville, nice young ladies of quality didn't speak to him, let alone want to date him.

Unwillingly, he faced the image of Cheyenne Whitney, which instantly flashed before his mind's eye. Okay, he conceded, Cheyenne was a lady of quality and she had spoken to him. She'd invited him to dinner too. And more.

He felt his heartbeat speed up and his body tense as the inevitable memories of their tempestuous kisses flooded him. The harder he tried to banish them—and her—from his mind, the more vivid and intense the images became.

It was disturbing, disconcerting. He was accustomed to being in complete control of himself, of his thoughts and actions, even his passions. He hated that this time he wasn't. He'd actually left Whitneyville a few days earlier than originally planned, because the temptation she presented had become almost too much to withstand.

Run out of town again, he thought glumly. Except this time it wasn't because he was despised by the town elite, it was because one of them found him desirable. The irony wasn't lost on him.

Whitneyville. Caleb frowned. He still spent entirely too much time thinking about the place. On that dark day fourteen years ago, when he'd been forced to leave his home and family, to quit school just three months shy of his high school graduation, he had vowed revenge on the town.

He walked over to the large map of the United States on the far wall of his office. Stuck into it were hundreds of colored pins locating each and every Dix-Mart store throughout the country. With great pleasure, Caleb poked in another pin, directly on top of the Whitneyville site.

He had won, for he'd seen the pattern time and time again. The big, new Dix-Mart with its vast array of merchandise and discount prices moved in and decimated the independent small-town businesses. Finances and demographics within the town changed dramatically within a very short time. Few townspeople were left unaffected by the sweeping shifts.

Come spring, with the opening of the latest Dix-Mart Discount City, Whitneyville would be changed irrevocably. And he, Dix-Mart's own C. W. Strong—Whitneyville's repudiated son—had set it all in motion by carefully selecting the town as the site. It had been a long time coming, fourteen years to be exact, but his promise of revenge would be fulfilled at last.

It had been an exhausting week for Cheyenne. It seemed like the entire sophomore class was particularly rebellious toward Shakespeare's *Julius Caesar*, and many students were not at all shy about expressing their displeasure with the mighty classic. On Friday night, she longed to change into comfortable clothes, make a big bowl of popcorn, and lie on the sofa while Brittany, Jeffrey, and Peppy watched their favorite lineup of television shows. Instead she had to dress for the Harpers' dinner party where she was to be not-so-subtly partnered with Ben Maitland.

She slipped on her pink turtleneck sweater dress, cinched in at the waist with a wide black belt, and low heels. It was a neat, classic style, but she knew she would be severely underdressed compared to the other women, who would be sporting new and expensive up-to-the-minute fashions. There had been a time in her life when that mattered to her. It didn't now.

Tricia was a gourmet cook and had prepared the elaborate dinner herself. It was, inevitably, superb. Ben Maitland was polite and attentive to Cheyenne, and she quickly realized that he was in the market for a steady companion. If she exerted even a little effort, it could be her. She wondered why the very thought made her want to run screaming from the house.

Conversation swirled around her at the dinner table. She tried to appear interested and alert, and gamely made attempts to participate. But she was restless and bored. Even in the midst of the talking, laughing crowd, a terrible loneliness gripped her. She felt depressed and alone, the way she'd been feeling for the past week and a half—ever since Caleb Strong's departure from Whitneyville.

There, at Tricia's well-appointed table, Cheyenne forced herself to face the truth she'd been assiduously avoiding. Though her encounters with Caleb had been brief, and intensely physical, he had evoked needs and emotions she could no longer repress and deny. She was dissatisfied with the sterility and predictability of her life. She wanted . . . She needed . . .

"Charades!" Tricia exclaimed. "Boys against the girls. We'll play out on the patio."

Cheyenne stared at her half-eaten dessert, a rich and sumptuous chocolate mousse. Didn't she feel a nasty headache coming on? She decided that she did and quickly made her apologies to Tricia, who tried desperately to convince her to stay.

Cheyenne was far more desperate to go. Ben, unfortunately, insisted on walking the short distance to her house with her. He was concerned and solicitous about her sudden illness, and she felt guilty because she wasn't sick at all. It was the threat of charades that had done it. She might have made it through the party if it hadn't included that particular game. She was *living* a charade, that of a heartbroken young widow, mourning the loss of her beloved husband and perfect marriage. A sham, all of it. She'd had it with charades.

Talking desultorily, she and Ben mounted the wide front porch steps of her house. "Tonight has been the most fun I've had since coming home to Whitneyville," he said smoothly. "It's a pleasure to meet you again, all grown-up, Cheyenne." He took a step closer to her and smiled invitingly.

Cheyenne quickly turned and plunged her key in the lock. Before she could turn it, the door was opened for her. By Caleb Strong. He was standing in the doorway, wearing his usual jeans and T-shirt, his lips curled into that sardonic smirk he passed off as a smile.

"Party break up early?" he asked.

Her jaw dropped, and she stared at him as if he were an apparition. "Caleb!" she gasped, and for one unguarded moment her face lit up as pure joy blazed through her.

And then, an awful thought struck her. "Has something happened to Joni Lynn?" she cried.

Caleb lounged against the doorjamb, his arms folded. The dark T-shirt exposed the muscular strength of those arms and, of course, the deadly cobra with its beady eyes and awesome fangs. "Joni Lynn is fine. I'm waiting for her to get off work. It seemed stupid to keep your baby-sitter while I was here, so I paid her and sent her home. The kids are asleep," he added. "I put them to bed an hour ago."

"Mrs. Merrit isn't feeling well," Ben said. "I think you'd better leave so she can get some rest." The hostility in his tone was unmistakable.

"If Mrs. Merrit wants me to leave, she'll tell me herself," Caleb said, his eyes as cold and deadly as his voice.

The animosity radiating between the two men was palpable and unnerving. Instinctively, Cheyenne interceded to smooth things over. "I'm sorry, I've been remiss in not making introductions. Ben, this is—"

"We know each other," Ben interrupted. "What I'd like to know is why you're back in Whitneyville, Strong. And more particularly, what are you doing *here*?"

"I guess you'll have to keep on wondering, Benji." Caleb flashed a chilling smile, then turned to Cheyenne. "That's what they used to call him in school. Benji. Like the dog in the movie."

Ben made a strange sort of growl, and Cheyenne had to stifle a nervous giggle. She sensed that a joke about the canine-type noise he'd just made and his old nickname wouldn't be appreciated at this time.

"I should have remembered that you two were in the same high school class," she said diplomatically.

"We were until he dropped out." Ben smiled smugly. "You left town immediately afterward, didn't you, Strong? You didn't graduate. I was the class salutatorian."

His tone was baiting, and Cheyenne felt a strange urge to protect Caleb from Ben Maitland's cruel jibes. Reflexively, she moved closer to Caleb. He hardly seemed to notice her, though. His eyes, narrowed and intent, were fixed on Ben.

"Are you aware that my sister Crystal's seventeen-year-old daughter lives right here, in the Whitney house?" That look in Caleb's eyes belied his nonchalant tone. "Her name is Joni Lynn Strong."

Ben uttered a curse, and Cheyenne stared at him in surprise. Gentlemen did not use such language in the presence of a lady. Her gaze darted from Ben's flushed, furious face to Caleb's composed, taunting one. The sickening possibility of a fight breaking out right there on her front porch seemed alarmingly real.

Once again, she tried to play the diplomatic peacemaker. "Ben is working in the Whitneyville Bank now," she said brightly, "and his older brother Graham is president, as their father and grandfather were."

Threatening silence continued to loom between the two men. Desperately, she made another stab at diversion. "As a matter of fact, we were talking about the bank at dinner tonight. It's the one institution here in town that is welcoming the new Dix-Mart with open arms, because of Dix-Mart's policy of allowing the local bank to handle its payroll and any local financial transactions. That will mean from six to ten million dollars a year in business for Whitneyville Bank. Did I get those facts right, Ben?" she asked, appealing to him more for peace than information.

"Is that so?" Caleb said before Ben could utter a word. "The Maitlands expect Whitneyville Bank to handle Dix-Mart's payroll?" He laughed, appearing genuinely amused.

Cheyenne stared at him, perplexed. She hadn't been trying to be funny.

Ben was not laughing either. "Why is Crystal Strong's daughter living with you, Cheyenne?" he demanded. His face was pinched, his tone agitated. "It's quite . . . unorthodox, you know."

"It's also none of your business, Benji," Caleb said, his shark's smile making Cheyenne shiver. He looked capable of anything when he was smiling that way, his eyes as hard as blue diamonds.

He turned his piercing gaze on her. "If you aren't feeling well, it's time for you to come inside and lie down."

Her heart lurched. Actually, it felt as if it had jumped the whole way into her throat. Caleb's words were possessive, his gaze frankly sexual. One could be excused for believing that he intended to lie down with her when she went inside. A covert glance at Ben's scowling face told her that *he* believed that.

What she should do, of course, was send both men on their way. Cheyenne was fully aware of that. If she went inside with Caleb, a vengeful Ben Maitland—rejected for a *Strong!*—would return to the party and tell the other guests whom she was entertaining. At night. Alone, while her children slept.

The Whitneyville grapevine was amazingly efficient. By tomorrow, the news would be all over town. "Not even being a Whitney could salvage your reputation if—heaven forbid—you were linked with *him!*" Tricia had said. She was undoubtedly right.

Cheyenne's eyes met Caleb's. He was watching her, his expression enigmatic. Did he want her to come with him? She couldn't tell. He was giving nothing away.

Her body throbbed in rhythm with her heartbeat. For the past week and a half she had been thinking of him, dreaming of him, and now he was here.

If she were to send him away, her reputation would remain intact and she could safely continue in her role as the town figurehead. Ben would inevitably call her for a first date and then a second, and they could pursue the same kind of conventional, socially approved, passionless relationship she had carried on with Evan Merrit for seven years.

She pressed her palms to her flushed cheeks. She couldn't look at either man as she slowly walked toward the door. "I'll go inside now," she said, her voice little more than a whisper. "Good night, Ben."

Seven

Cheyenne hurried inside, keeping her eyes straight ahead. She heard but didn't see Ben's immediate exit. His exclamation of angry disapproval echoed in her ears as she walked on into the middle of her living room. Peppy lay on the floor in front of the window, sleeping. He opened one eye, saw her, and promptly closed it again.

"Are you really feeling sick?"

She turned at the sound of Caleb's voice. He was standing on the threshold of the room.

"No," she said softly. "I only said that because I wanted to leave Tricia's party and come home."

His stare was piercing, penetrating, as if he were trying to look inside her very soul. "Because you wanted to be alone with Maitland?"

"Good heavens, no!"

"Are you dating him?"

She shook her head. "He just walked me here from Tricia's house. This is the first time I've seen him in years. He only recently moved back to town to work in the family bank."

"Which they think is in for a windfall from Dix-Mart." He shook his head and gave a short, sharp laugh. He looked hard and dangerous as he strode into the living room. "If you had hopes of dating Maitland, you blew them sky-high by sending him away and coming inside with me, Cheyenne."

Just hearing him say her name gave her a thrill. "I know," she said softly. She forced herself to meet his eyes, and gasped at the glowing arousal she saw there. Breathlessly, she watched him walk toward her.

"There is bad blood between the Maitland brothers and me," he said. "To Master Benji's way of thinking, you just chose a Strong over him." He stood before her, gazing down at her. "Do you realize that?"

"Yes," she whispered.

They stared at each other for a long, tension-charged moment. The fire in his eyes sparked a sensual heat deep within her. When he reached for her, she went immediately into his arms. She moaned softly when his mouth, hot and urgent, claimed hers in a hungry kiss.

She clung to him, kissing him with all the passion he had awakened within her, passion that had built and grown during his absence and now exploded into feverish need.

They kissed again and again, each kiss growing deeper, more intimate, more demanding. He cupped her swollen breasts, and she pressed closer, pushing herself against his palm. His big, warm hand felt so good, so strong. When his thumb traced a lazy circle around the taut peak of her nipple, she whimpered and rubbed sinuously against him. His thigh was between hers, moving slowly back and forth, exerting an exquisite pressure, and she shuddered at the pleasure he evoked.

Her complete and uninhibited response obliterated Caleb's customary cool control. His body pulsed with a need too powerful to be dismissed as mere desire. He wanted her, only her, and he wanted her with every fiber of his being.

Without lifting his mouth from hers, he scooped

her up in his arms and carried her to the sofa. Her senses heightened to fever-pitch awareness, Cheyenne was attuned to every detail, to the feel of the worn, cool chintz against her back and the contrasting warm, heavy weight of Caleb as he came down on top of her. The musky scent of him filled her nostrils as his tongue plunged deep in her mouth.

She arched into him, her nails digging into his shoulders in a reflexive, primal signal of passion that made him groan with a fierce urgency. He shifted his weight, lying between her thighs, opening her legs wider with his own. The pliable fabric of her dress accommodatingly glided up.

Liquid fire burned through Cheyenne's veins. She cried out and writhed against him, her hands stroking greedily, possessively, over the hard length of his back, daring even to touch his taut buttocks. She could feel the full force of his masculinity, hard and throbbing against the most feminine, most vulnerable part of her, and she quivered with arousal and need.

With a natural abandon that previously had been foreign to her, she flexed her knees and languorously lifted her legs, fitting them snugly over his hips. Her skirt rode higher, but she neither noticed nor cared. Her mind was reeling from the feel of Caleb's hands smoothing over the long length of her legs.

She was wearing rose-tinted panty hose, which complemented her dress well. But as his hands glided along her calves, her thighs, explored the curve of her hips, she wished that she wasn't wearing functional panty hose but a sexy, alluring garter belt and stockings. She'd always considered such items too embarrassingly frivolous and seductive for her even to own, let alone wear. But she wanted them now, to wear for Caleb. To entice him, to incite him.

Her eyes flew open at her shockingly wanton thoughts. She drew in a sharp little breath as her gaze met his. His intense look was as scorching as his hands. It was both unnerving and thrilling to know that he had seen her writhing beneath him in the throes of passion, that he knew beyond a doubt the sensual power he had over her, that he possessed such intimate knowledge of her.

Still holding her gaze with his, he slipped one long finger beneath the waistband of her panty hose, only to encounter the elastic waistband of her white cotton panties. A slight smile curved his lips. "You're well armored, sweetheart," he said lightly, then audaciously slipped his palm inside her panties to stroke the soft bare skin of her belly.

Cheyenne sucked in her breath, and her eyelids dropped closed as she felt his thumb circle her navel in a sensual, rhythmic motion, the same that he had used to stimulate her nipples. She wanted him to touch her there again. Her breasts were swollen and aching, her nipples so tight and sensitive, she almost pleaded for his touch. A provocative heat stabbed her belly and twisted downward to burn and ache between her thighs. She wanted to feel his hand there to. . . .

"You're hot, baby, so hot," he breathed, his mouth against her ear. "I want you so much, I'm almost ready to take you right here."

His words inflamed her, and she cried his name. Her mouth groped blindly for his, wanting, needing to feel it crushing hers. Caleb recognized her loss of control and suddenly, unexpectedly, felt incredibly protective of her. Though he burned for the sweet release her luscious body would provide, he forced himself to put a brake on his surging passion.

"Sweetie, we can't." He sighed raggedly. "Not here. Not now. Your kids are upstairs and could wake up and come down at any time, and Joni Lynn is due back soon. Even the dog is right here in the room with us!"

His words barely penetrated the sensual cloud enveloping Cheyenne. It wasn't until he sat upright on the sofa, taking her with him, that their meaning became clear. No more lovemaking. Not here, not now.

She opened her eyes and stared dazedly at him. She was sitting on his lap, straddling him, her skirt hiked high. And he was still watching her. His knowing gaze, which had thrilled her only moments before, now made her flinch. She was mortified by her wanton behavior and loss of control. *What if Brittany or Jeffrey or Joni Lynn had appeared and observed the two of them entangled on the sofa?* She hadn't given that possibility a thought. But Caleb had.

Her face flushed with shame, and she frantically tried to pull her skirt down. When her hand brushed the hard swell of his masculinity by mistake, she gasped and he groaned. She made a desperate, awkward attempt to escape, but Caleb's hands clamped around her waist with viselike strength, keeping her firmly astride him in that exceedingly sexual position.

"Stop struggling and keep still," he muttered.

"Let me go," she whispered, gulping back a sob.

"Cheyenne, for Pete's sakes, don't cry."

"I'm not crying!" She was aroused, emotionally and physically, and sexually frustrated. It was convenient to use him as an outlet for all those charged feelings, and she did. "I would never cry over *you*, Caleb Strong!"

He lifted his hand to her face and traced the path of one renegade tear that had escaped from her eye and trickled down her cheek. "You wouldn't, huh?"

She shook her head vigorously.

"Look, I know what I did was rotten, getting us both all heated up and then pulling back," he said bluntly. "But—"

"Don't!" She tried to scramble off his lap again, and this time, almost succeeded.

Still he caught her before she could get up and held

her fast. She clasped her legs tightly together and gave her skirt another desperate tug. Although she was still trapped on his lap, at least her position was no longer as provocative, and she tried to take small comfort in that.

"I didn't come here for a fast lay on the sofa, Cheyenne."

Caleb had tried to tell himself that he had come to see Joni Lynn, but he knew only too well that his need to see Cheyenne had become too powerful to resist. Not even the dampening news that she was out for the evening had daunted him. He'd stayed with her children, waiting for her return.

"It's crazy." He frowned, confused and bemused. "The moment I started kissing you, things got out of hand. I can't explain it other than you seem to have that kind of effect on me. It's, well, it's damn mystifying!"

It was also unnerving, disconcerting, and downright scary. No woman had ever affected him this way before, though he wasn't about to admit *that* to her. She had entirely too much power over him as it was.

He thought of Lindsey Carroll, the young woman he'd met at the Ralburns' dinner party a week ago. She had been gorgeous and sweet, but her eager kiss had not moved him at all. Feeling desperate, he'd taken her out once more, only to admit the obvious to himself. Lindsey Carroll could not supplant Cheyenne Whitney Merrit in his thoughts or in his dreams, nor could the other two women he'd dated the past week in sheer self-defense.

Cheyenne stared at him. His agitated admission struck a chord in her. She knew exactly the way he felt. "You have that kind of effect on me too," she confessed in a whisper. "And you're right, it *is* mystifying. I've never felt—that is, no one has ever made me feel . . ." She paused and gulped. "The way you do."

His hand cupped the nape of her neck, and he

pulled her down so that she was reclining against him, her head resting on his chest. "So what are we going to do about it, Miss Cheyenne?"

She could hear the rapid beat of his heart against her ear. His arms were wrapped firmly around her, and his manhood, full and hard, pulsed against her bottom. She laid her hands on his, which were linked over her stomach. She felt surrounded by him, protected and possessed. And she was positively stunned to hear herself blurt out, "Go to the Magic Carpet?"

He laughed softly. "I suppose I deserved that one, didn't I?"

He thought she was kidding, making a joking reference to when he'd tried to whisk her off to the motel. What if he knew she was utterly serious? Cheyenne wasn't sure if she was relieved or not that he had misinterpreted her question.

"You were right to say no to me that day," he went on. "I shouldn't have tried to hustle you into some quick sex at the Magic Carpet. You—" He cleared his throat, his face slightly flushed. "—you deserve more than that, Cheyenne."

She lay quietly in his arms, more confused than she'd ever been in her life. Just when she'd reached the conclusion that it wasn't so wrong to go to his motel room with him, he seemed to have concluded the opposite. She waited for him to say more, hoping to pick up some cue from him on what to say next. But he was silent, one hand lightly stroking her hair, the other kneading the hollow of her waist.

Response rippled through her. It was difficult to remain still. She wanted to stretch languidly under his hands, to feel them touching her all over. A syrupy warmth pooled deep within her. She sighed.

"I missed you," she murmured. She wanted him to know, feeling too close to him to hold anything back. "I didn't know when you were coming back. Or if you would want to see me again." A shiver ran through her.

"It certainly wasn't part of my original plans," he said honestly.

That was an understatement, he thought, especially after spending all this time attempting to put her out of his mind. He didn't particularly believe in fate, but *something* out of the ordinary seemed to be at work here. Just as he was about to put the screws to Whitneyville, who should land in his lap—literally—but Little Miss Whitney herself! Was it fate, opportunity, luck, or chance? He couldn't begin to fathom it.

"But here I am," he added, sounding a bit addled. His fingers glided through her silky hair, and he inhaled the fresh, clean scent of it.

Yes, here he was, back in Whitneyville to finalize the plans he'd set in motion years ago. To claim the revenge he'd dreamed of for fourteen long years. But his plans hadn't included holding a warm, submissive Cheyenne Whitney in his arms, the direct descendant of the founders of the town he hated more than any other place on earth.

"Here you are," Cheyenne echoed softly. She dared to raise her hand to his face and trace the strong line of his jaw. Boldly, she let her fingers stray closer to his mouth. He caught her hand and pressed his lips against her palm. She quivered.

"Are you staying at the Magic Carpet Motel again?" she asked breathlessly. "Joni Lynn told me it's your home away from home."

He arched his brows. "What else has Joni Lynn been telling you about me?"

"Nothing." Gathering all her courage, she added, "When I asked her about your job, she said that only the Strongs are allowed to know who you work for and what you do."

It was an obvious invitation for him to confide in her, and for a moment, Caleb considered it. Then he rejected the idea. As much as he wanted her sexually, and in spite of these inconvenient, troubling feelings of tenderness for her that kept getting in his way, he wasn't ready to trust her.

"That's right. Only the Strongs can know." He flashed a charming, teasing grin.

Cheyenne saw it for exactly what it was—an attempt to distance himself from her. He had no intention of revealing the truth about himself. Obviously the closeness she was feeling was one-sided. A wave of sadness swept through her.

Caleb saw the light fade from her eyes, the shadow cross her face. "Regrets?" he asked, and wished he felt as cool as he sounded. A frustrating ambivalence tore through him. He'd deliberately shut her out, yet he wanted her to be close and open with him. "Wishing you'd kicked me out and were sitting here with safe, respectable Benji Maitland instead?"

The very idea was revolting! he thought with horror. Suppose she really were wishing that?

Cheyenne stared at him thoughtfully. She felt the tension in his body, saw the muscle in his jaw twitch, watched his hand clench into a fist. He appeared to be gearing up for a quarrel. Another attempt to distance himself from her? Should she play it cool, and say yes, she wished Ben were there?

Perhaps it would be good strategy in a sexual war, but she just couldn't do it. She didn't want a war with him, she wanted . . . him. "I don't want Ben Maitland," she said flatly. "I wouldn't have invited him in, even if you hadn't been here."

"Just remember this." His voice was rough, his eyes blazing. "The day you start anything with a Maitland is the day I move my niece out of this house."

His intensity intrigued her. "Why do you and the Maitlands hate each other?" she asked, then couldn't resist adding, "Or is that another thing only the Strongs are allowed to know?"

"It's something the Maitlands wouldn't want you to know, something they've kept quiet for the past seventeen years." His voice grew hard. "But I believe you should know, since you've involved yourself with one of the Strongs—who also happens to be a Maitland."

She frowned, puzzled. "I don't think I understand."

"Joni Lynn is both a Strong and a Maitland, Cheyenne."

"What?" She bolted upright and gaped at him.

"Graham Maitland is Joni Lynn's father. I know it's impossible to believe that a secret could actually be kept in this town, but there it is." He smiled without mirth. "Not even Joni Lynn knows who her father is. Nobody knows but a few Strongs and a few Maitlands. And now you."

"Graham Maitland!" Cheyenne was stunned. "Why, he lives just two blocks up the street. My family has known his forever. I remember going to his wedding, when he married Polly Norwood, his high school sweetheart. I was eleven years old and I thought it was all so romantic, the beautiful bride in her white gown, the flowers and the music and the big reception afterward."

"Yeah, I remember that wedding, too, only not so fondly. The groom's one-year-old daughter wasn't included. The Maitlands refused to acknowledge her existence and, of course, Graham didn't tell his bride about his baby. As far as I know, he never has. I also remember when the happy young couple announced their engagement. It was just two weeks before Joni Lynn was born."

Dazed, Cheyenne stood up and walked to the window. She knew Graham and Polly Maitland as pillars of the community, a solid couple with two handsome, bright young sons. Except, Graham was really the father of three. He and Crystal Strong shared a child, a beautiful, bright daughter named Joni Lynn.

"It's hard to take in," she said shakily. The Maitlands were one of the most prestigious families in Whitneyville. There had never been a hint of scandal or a whisper of gossip about them. "How did it happen? I—I mean, why?"

"You mean why would a respectable young man from a good family take up with a trashy girl from the wrong side of the tracks?"

She whirled around to face him. "You know that's not what I meant. I love Joni Lynn, and I want to know how her parents got together and—and why they didn't stay together since they had a child."

"You want history." He sighed heavily. "Well, I'm the one who can give it to you. I remember every detail from that time only too well. Graham Maitland was twenty-three, back in town with a college degree, working at the family bank and feeling bored and rebellious. He hadn't wanted to come back to Whitneyville, but since he was crown prince of the Whitneyville Bank, he had no choice. Maybe he felt he had no choice about marrying his high school sweetheart, either, and he resented that too. My sister Crystal had just turned sixteen. She was as pretty as Joni Lynn, but not nearly as smart. She was gullible and restless, a prime target for a smooth rich boy's lines. Looking back, it's as if they were on a collision course. The result was Joni Lynn."

"Poor Crystal," Cheyenne said quietly.

"Yeah, poor deluded Crystal. She loved Graham Maitland and believed he loved her. He didn't, of course. He'd merely been using her. As soon as he found out she was pregnant, he couldn't dump her fast enough. I can still remember the expression on Crystal's face when she opened the *Whitneyville Gazette* and saw Maitland's engagement announcement. 'Their marriage will join two of Whitneyville's finest, oldest families,'" he quoted bitterly. "Of course, no mention was made of the prospective bridegroom's secret girlfriend who happened to be nine months pregnant."

"That's terrible! So cruel and unfair!" Cheyenne exclaimed. "Has Graham ever contributed to Joni Lynn's support?"

"He paid Crystal's hospital bill and gave her cash for the first couple years." Caleb smiled grimly. "He had to. I went to him and threatened to beat the hell out of him and tell the whole town about the baby if he didn't."

"You were only a boy, then," she said slowly. "But you took on the Maitlands?"

He shrugged. "There was nobody else to do it. Our dad would have, but he was dead. He'd drowned in a flash flood five years earlier. My grandfather was a drunk, and my uncles were weak and ineffectual and scared of the Maitlands. My mother was too tired and overworked to do much of anything but collapse on the sofa when she got home from work. We badly needed money to pay the hospital bill and support the baby, and I made sure we got it."

Cheyenne felt a thrill of pride. "That was a wonderful thing to do, Caleb."

"Not so wonderful. Once I left town, the arrangement fell apart. Maitland never paid Crystal another cent for the child."

She crossed the room to sit beside him on the sofa. "Caleb, why did you leave? I've often wondered why you quit school so near to graduation."

"That's explained in Part Two of Caleb Strong versus the Maitlands. Do you really want to hear the entire saga?" His voice was light, but his eyes were cold.

He would make an unsparing adversary, Cheyenne thought. And a formidable ally. She nodded.

"The year Ben Maitland and I were seniors in high school," he continued, "Crystal had a waitressing job at Oakes Diner. In the spring, she began coming home in tears because Benji-boy was stopping in the diner and making lewd jokes and remarks to her. Seems the little creep had developed a yen for his older brother's former flame. It wasn't long before the remarks escalated to pressure and threats. Ben told Crystal if she didn't put out for him, his family would go to court to have her declared an unfit mother and the baby would be taken away from her. I seriously doubt that the older Maitlands would have done any such thing. They'd made it plain they didn't care if Joni Lynn lived or died, but Crystal was hysterical. She was torn between giving in to him or killing herself or maybe both."

"Oh, no," Cheyenne whispered.

"Crystal was nineteen years old, young and poor and powerless. A born victim." Caleb's voice was bitter. "When she finally confided in me, I told her to arrange a meeting with Ben in the grove. He showed up, thinking he was going to score. Guess who was there instead?"

"You."

He nodded. "Me. I have to admit that back in those days, I was a dirty fighter who showed no mercy. I also had the element of surprise to my advantage."

"You beat the hell out of him," Cheyenne guessed hopefully.

"Yeah, I did. Looking back from an adult's perspective, I was way too rough. I could've killed him. Actually, I came mighty close. I drove him home in his car and left him in it unconscious, in the driveway."

Cheyenne smiled widely. "Oh, Caleb, I'm so glad you did! He deserved it!"

"Bloodthirsty little thing, aren't you?" he said with a slight chuckle. "But I learned a valuable lesson that night, one I've never forgotten. Physical violence isn't an effective means of revenge. It can backfire, like it did on me. I thought I'd solved our problems, but I'd actually made them worse."

"What happened?" She had a sinking feeling in her stomach. Subsequent events had proven that the Strongs had lost to the Maitlands, and she wanted to cry out at the unfairness of it all.

"Later that night, the police came to our house, accompanied by Graham, his father, and their lawyer. I was to be arrested for a whole list of crimes, ranging from attempted murder to car theft."

"That's not fair! You were protecting your sister!"

"I went about it the wrong way, Cheyenne. I know now that the most effective means of revenge is either to attack an enemy financially, destroy a carefully built reputation, or both. Hit them there, and you've got your revenge. In the long run, beating up Ben cost me and my family more, hurt us more, than it ever did him."

"Did you go to jail?" she asked numbly.

"Surprisingly, no. I guess there was too much danger of the truth coming out about Graham and Crystal and Joni Lynn if word got out about the fight. But I was too young and dumb to see that as the ace it was. I let the lawyer offer me an alternative to going to jail."

"You had to leave town," she concluded sadly. "Even though it meant dropping out of school and not graduating."

He nodded. "The deal was that if I agreed to leave town immediately, that very night, charges wouldn't be filed. I was ordered to stay away from Whitneyville for a minimum of five years, and when and if I ever returned, I was never to go near any of the Maitlands. If I reneged on the agreement, there would be hell to pay. All charges against me would be reinstated, they'd see to it that my mother and my uncles lost their jobs, Crystal would be declared an unfit mother. I also remember one cop mentioning that his brother-in-law was a volunteer fireman, and if any of the Strongs' houses were to catch fire, the fire engine might not make it in time. It was a direct threat and I knew it. I left Whitneyville that night."

"Caleb, I'm so sorry." Impulsively, she put her arms around him and hugged him tight. "You were just a kid. What did you do? Where did you go?"

"We'll save that for another time." He patted her hand, then stood up and stepped away from her. Reminiscing was dangerous, and he usually avoided it. But being back in Whitneyville seemed to undermine his resolutions. Seeing Ben Maitland for the first time in fourteen years had been disturbing, and seeing him with Cheyenne had been enough to unhinge him. Which probably explained why he'd broken his long vow of silence and told her about Joni Lynn. He'd been temporarily unhinged.

He stared at Cheyenne askance. She had an incredible power over him. He might end up telling her everything if he stayed. The temptation of her soft arms and admiring eyes and sweet, sweet mouth were risks he couldn't take, not now.

He wanted her. When he'd been lying with her on the sofa, he'd been on the verge of *needing* her, ferociously. That troubled him. His strongest emotion had always been anger, and since that unforgettable night when he'd been run out of town, he had learned to channel that anger into a steely, ruthless ambition. There was no place in his life for explosive, uncontrollable feelings. This hunger he'd developed for Cheyenne Whitney did not belong in his plans.

"Caleb?"

Her voice filtered into his reverie. He glanced at her to find her watching him. No, he wouldn't succumb to her again. "It's time for me to leave, babe." He started toward the door, aware that his exit wasn't the smoothest he'd ever made. He was too shook up to be smooth.

She made no attempt to follow him. "I just wondered if you stayed away from Whitneyville for those five years," she said quietly.

He paused and nodded. "I didn't dare not to. I was nobody then, and I'd put my whole family's welfare at risk."

"It must have been hard, not seeing them for such a long time."

He shrugged. "We got around it. I'd come into Smithboro a couple times a year, and the whole family would drive over and meet me there. When I started making money, I'd rent some rooms at the hotel there and we'd have a regular reunion. I've always had a fondness for that little town. Actually, I didn't set foot in Whitneyville for nearly twelve years, by my own choice." He turned again to leave, but again her voice halted him.

"Caleb? Do you think that Ben Maitland will make trouble for you and your family now that he's seen you back in town?"

Caleb laughed. "I'd like to see him try. I'm not the powerless young kid I was fourteen years ago, Cheyenne. It would be a big mistake for anyone to try to cross me now."

He sounded so cold and steely, a dangerous force to be reckoned with. She gazed at him, feeling vaguely troubled. Who was Caleb Strong and what was he doing there? She wanted to ask him, but she knew he wouldn't tell her. Only the Strongs were allowed to know about him. In that, he'd made them the most exclusive group in Whitneyville. Her golden names of Whitney and Merrit guaranteed her admission to wherever she wanted to go in town, but they didn't provide entry to the secrets of the Strongs. This time *she* was the outsider, and oh, how she wanted in!

She walked him to the front door, hostess to guest, the etiquette ingrained. "Shall I tell Joni Lynn that you'll be by to see her tomorrow?" she asked politely, though her mind was racing as fast as her heart.

"Yes," he replied, equally preoccupied.

"What time shall I tell her? Just in case she asks."

"How's eleven-thirty?"

"Fine. Uh, that is, I'm sure that will be all right with Joni Lynn."

He stepped out onto the porch. She followed immediately. *She didn't want him to go!* "I didn't see your motorcycle when I came in," she said quickly. She was stalling him, and she guessed he probably knew it. She didn't care.

"It's halfway up the block. The old bat across the street was peering out her window when I rode up, and I didn't want to create a scandal by parking in front of your house."

She folded her arms across her chest. "As far as I'm concerned, you can park wherever you want."

"Brave words, little girl. But you'll have enough trouble to contend with if Benji decides to muddy your name by coupling it with mine. Do you think you can handle it?"

"I'm not afraid of a little gossip!" More brave words. She'd lived her life to avoid gossip—and suddenly it seemed so suffocating, so unbearably stultifying. Her safe, secure world of Whitneyville seemed as restrictive as a prison.

"Of course you're not," Caleb said dryly. Impulsively, he leaned down and brushed his mouth over hers. He hadn't intended to kiss her at all, but once his lips touched hers, he decided it would be a quick, perfunctory, *impersonal* kiss.

Then Cheyenne melted against him, and her fingers tangled in his hair, holding his head to hers. Her mouth opened under his, and with a daring, seductive prowess she never dreamed she possessed, she slipped her tongue into his mouth. His arms came around to encircle her, and he pulled her tightly against him.

The kiss was long and deep and devastating. The passion they had managed to put on hold a short while earlier, flared and raged anew.

They were so absorbed in each other, they ignored the canine whine from inside the house. But when Peppy flung himself at the screen door and began to bark, they slowly and reluctantly drew apart.

Cheyenne had to remind herself to breathe. The world seemed to be spinning dizzily around her, and her body throbbed with urgency. A quick glance at Caleb confirmed that he was in similar straits.

"Peppy strikes again," he muttered. "That mutt has incredibly lousy timing."

Peppy wagged his tail and barked.

"I'll put him outside in the backyard," Cheyenne said huskily.

Caleb didn't trust himself to speak. He had an unnerving hunch that if he were to open his mouth, it would be to volunteer to walk the dog for her. And that, of course, would mean prolonging this visit, spending more time with her, kissing her again, wanting her more and more. . . .

With a wave of his hand, he bounded down the porch stairs. Tonight's visit had confirmed that he was much too vulnerable to the charms of Cheyenne Whitney Merrit. He *had* to stay away from her. He would take care to do so while he remained in Whitneyville. Fleeing for his bachelor life, Caleb sped off into the night.

Eight

"Is this where Uncle Caleb lives, Mommy?" Brittany asked as Cheyenne led her and Jeffrey from their car to Room 9 at the Magic Carpet Motel.

"Only sometimes," Cheyenne said, clinging to their hands. She glanced down at the two of them, so cute in their little sneakers and jeans and matching red, white, and blue jerseys. She'd tied up Brittany's braids in loops with bright red ribbons. How could anyone resist them, especially a man like Caleb, who so obviously enjoyed children?

She cast a quick nervous glance at her own outfit, pale blue jeans and a blue chambray blouse a few shades darker than the jeans. Though she rarely wore jeans, she'd always owned a pair in case an occasion required them. This was definitely one of those occasions. She wanted to appear approachable and down-home, as far from Caleb's elitist Whitneyville image of her as she could possibly get.

"Look!" Jeffrey exclaimed. "The doors are purple and red and purple and red and purple—"

"Yes, we see," Cheyenne interrupted, when it became clear that he was bent on naming the colors of all the doors, which were painted in alternating garish shades of red and purple. A misguided attempt to conjure up a Middle Eastern flavor as a tie-in with the motel's name, perhaps? Whatever the motivation, the doors were blindingly ostentatious.

"I like Uncle Caleb," Brittany confided. "I'm going to give him a big hug."

"I'm sure he'll like that very much, Brittany," Cheyenne said, and a nagging pang of guilt assailed her once again. It had been striking at regular intervals since she'd concocted this plan the night before.

She should be ashamed of herself for using little children in her pursuit of Caleb Strong, she scolded herself for at least the tenth time. But shame ran a poor second to need. She'd seen the expression on his face when he'd bolted from her house last night. He might want her—and she'd felt his body's hard, unmistakable evidence of that—but he was determined to stay away from her.

She knew why for she was beginning to know him, to understand him. To Caleb's way of thinking, a Whitney, though not as maleficent as a Maitland, nevertheless represented the powerful ruling class of the town that had so grievously wronged his family.

Caleb did not intend to see her anymore, she had no doubts about that. Nor did she doubt the power of his iron will to follow through on his resolution. Unless she took drastic action to alter the situation, it would be over between them before it had really begun. She couldn't let that happen!

Jeffrey's voice broke into her turbulent thoughts. "Can Uncle Caleb go to McDonald's with us?"

She swallowed. "If he wants to."

She quickly knocked on the bright red door of Room 9, before she completely lost her nerve. She had never pursued a man, had never lain awake plotting and planning how to inveigle her way into his life. Not until now. It was terrifying. If he . . .

The door opened. Caleb's eyes widened at the sight of them. Cheyenne's widened at the sight of him. She had never seen him dressed like this before, in khaki slacks and a yellow knit polo shirt, well-worn deck shoes without socks. He looked preppy, someone out of a Ralph Lauren ad, rather than his usual self. Even his tattoo was covered by the longer sleeves of his shirt.

"Hi, Uncle Caleb!" Jeffrey chirped, breaking the momentary silence. "We came to see you," he added importantly.

Brittany cast her mother an uncertain glance, then determinedly stepped forward and wrapped her small arms around Caleb's legs in the aforementioned hug.

Cheyenne's knees were rubbery. When Caleb smiled and picked up both children, settling each on a hip, she breathed a shaky sigh of relief. Though she had been counting on him warmly welcoming the children, she'd feared the possibility that he wouldn't. She didn't know what she would have done if that had happened.

"Well, this is a surprise." He remained in the doorway for a moment, blocking it, then quickly pulled the door closed behind him.

Cheyenne felt a thunderous roaring in her ears. It was obvious he didn't want them to come into his room! Because he had someone in there? *A woman?*

His eyes connected briefly with hers, then he immediately turned his attention back to the children.

Cheyenne was aghast. How was she going to gracefully get out of there? "We're on our way to lunch," she said quickly, "and we stopped by because Joni Lynn had to leave for work earlier than eleven-thirty, so we thought we'd save you the trip to our house."

It wasn't a complete fabrication. Joni Lynn really was going to her job at the ice-cream shop earlier than the prearranged visit. Except Cheyenne had known the day before that Joni Lynn would be gone when she'd told Caleb that eleven-thirty was fine. She hadn't wanted him to come to the house, only to leave with Joni Lynn. She'd needed an excuse to come to the motel so she and the children could entice him to join them. She needed time with him, time to con-

vince him that there was no class conflict between
them. Time to convince him that a Whitney just
might be the perfect partner for a Strong.

It had seemed like a good, feasible plan. She just
hadn't considered that he might not be alone upon
their arrival. "Since our message is delivered, we'll be
on our way," she managed to choke out. "Let's go,
kids." Though Caleb was still holding the children,
she started back to the car.

"I want to go in your house, Uncle Caleb," Jeffrey
said. He pointed to the red door. "In there."

"It's only a room, Jeffrey," Caleb said, "and it's a real
mess." In truth, the room was as clean as when he'd
checked in the day before. He'd never been a slob. But
his computer and stacks of paperwork were on the
makeshift desk, and he wasn't ready to break the
secret of his identity. Not yet.

"Jeffrey, we have to go. Mr. Strong is busy," Cheyenne called frantically. There was a women in that
room, she knew it. Last night, Caleb had gone from
her to another woman to seek the physical satisfaction he'd denied them both. She felt like raging, she
felt like crying. If she didn't get away from there
soon . . .

"Uncle Caleb, would you take me to Kimmy's house
today?" Brittany asked, following up on a conversation she'd had with him the previous evening when
Caleb had replaced the baby-sitter with himself. The
dream of playing with one hundred Barbie dolls was
not lightly set aside.

"Brittany, Jeffrey, come along!" Cheyenne sounded
desperate, even to her own ears. Her children were
doing exactly what she'd hoped they would do, to get
Caleb to stay with them. Unfortunately, it was the
last thing she wanted now.

"We're going to McDonald's for lunch," Jeffrey said.
"Do you want to come, Uncle Caleb?"

Cheyenne heaved an impatient, exasperated sigh.

"No, he does not want to come, Jeffrey. But if *you* don't come right now, we'll go straight home and—"

"I'll go to lunch with you," Caleb cut in. "Let's go." Still carrying both children, he walked to Cheyenne's small blue Escort.

Brittany and Jeffrey were pleased. "Then can we go to Kimmy's?" the little girl asked hopefully.

"Sure," he said. "We'll all go over after lunch. I'll drive," he added to Cheyenne. "Give me the keys."

Their eyes met, his amused and knowing; hers, angry and hurt—and now confused. "You can't come with us," she said unsteadily. "What about your— your—" She inclined her head toward the room. This was a delicate subject to broach with two innocent and inquisitive children listening in.

"My what?" he asked blandly.

"Your friend in your room," she muttered, her teeth clenched.

Caleb set the children down and opened the car door for them. They clambered inside.

"There's nobody in there, Miss Cheyenne." He smiled a lazy, insolent smile. "What did you think, that I had Penny Sherwood stashed in the closet? Or perhaps in the shower?"

Cheyenne blushed and looked at the ground.

"Aha! You did." He walked around to the driver's side where she was standing. "Give me the keys, Cheyenne."

"It was very obvious that you didn't want us in that room," she said defensively.

He shrugged. "Like I told Jeffrey, it's a mess."

Could it really be that simple? She stared at him helplessly, wanting so much to believe him, yet unable to dispel the threatening doubts.

"Don't chicken out now, Cheyenne. You've accomplished what you set out to do. I'm here with you and the kids. We're going to lunch and then to my sister's place. You'll be with me all day—just what you wanted."

"Oh!" Cheyenne was appalled that he had seen through her so easily. And that he had the nerve to call her on it! "I—I was only trying to be helpful," she insisted, spluttering. "I thought I'd save you a trip to my house."

"Cheyenne, I know what's going on. I've been chased by women before."

Her mouth dropped open. She was certain her face was turning as purple as one of those hideous doors. "I am not chasing you!" She tersely accentuated each word.

He merely laughed. "Hmm-mm."

"I have never chased a man before in my life, and I'm not about to start now!"

Jeffrey chose that minute to catapult himself into the front seat and lean on the car horn. "Beep, beep," he shouted out the window, in case the horn didn't make his point. "Time to go!"

"You heard the little guy." Caleb reached over and took the car keys from her hand. "Move it, Mommy." He almost gave her bottom a playful swat, but she jumped away just in time.

He was grinning, and she was seething. *He'd accused her of chasing him!* Even worse, he was absolutely right. For a moment, Cheyenne stood stock-still, watching him climb behind the steering wheel. Brittany and Jeffrey buckled themselves into the small backseat.

Caleb leaned out the window. "C'mon, baby, get in," he said in a coaxing, seductive tone that affected her like a caress. Desire shot through her, as swift and sharp as a laser beam. He probably knew that too, she through grimly. He knew entirely too much about women. He was light-years ahead of her in experience.

But what choice did she have, except to get in the car? He and the children were already firmly entrenched there. Mortified beyond measure, she climbed in and allowed him to drive them to McDonald's, located in a strip of fast-food restaurants on Route Six, midway between Whitneyville and Smithboro.

They passed the Dix-Mart construction site along the way. The heavy machinery and construction crew were hard at work, Caleb noted. He had visited them earlier that morning and complimented them on their progress.

At McDonald's, Caleb insisted upon paying for their lunches, increasing Cheyenne's discomfort. "Next, I suppose you'll accuse me of deliberately sponging free meals from you," she hissed under her breath as they walked to a booth together. Brittany and Jeffrey were outside, climbing on the jungle gym in the enclosed playground.

"No." He shook his head. "Your plan wasn't that detailed. You didn't think beyond being with me."

"Will you stop that? I'm not chasing you!"

"Didn't I mention that it's very flattering? How remiss of me."

He was teasing her now, but Cheyenne was feeling too vulnerable to appreciate the humor. She was as unused to his directness as she was to the strength of the emotions he evoked within her.

She bit down on her quivering lower lip, embarrassed and annoyed with herself. Why did she have to get so emotional around Caleb? She'd never shed a tear over Evan Merrit during the ten interminable years she was with him. "I know you don't want to be with me," she murmured. "As soon as the children have finished eating, we'll go home, and I promise not to ever b-bother you again."

He set the tray down on the table. "Maybe that's a promise I don't want you to make," he said softly.

She couldn't look at him. She kept her gaze affixed to the bright, colorful pictures on the children's cardboard meal boxes. "I know you didn't want to see me again," she said, casting subterfuge and strategy aside. They hadn't worked. Caleb had seen right through them, through her. She had nothing more to lose. "I knew it when you left last night. I shouldn't have come to your room today, I—"

"Since you're being honest, I'll be honest with you," he cut in. "You're right. When I left last night I had no intention of seeing you again."

"Because I'm a Whitney," she said sadly.

"There's that, of course. But mostly because I want you more than I've ever wanted a woman in my life. I'm having trouble handling that, Cheyenne."

She looked up at him, not knowing what to say. His admission sent her spirits soaring. Her throat tightened with excitement. She no longer felt like bursting into tears.

"I have feelings for you that I've never experienced before," he went on quietly. "It's just too intense. And good Lord, we've never even been to bed! If that ever happens . . ."

"You mean *when* it happens," she blurted out, feeling paradoxically bold and uncertain, brave and afraid.

He arched his brows. "So you think it's a foregone conclusion? That sooner or later we're going to end up in bed together?" He smiled wickedly. "Once again, you surprise me, Miss Cheyenne. A few minutes ago you freaked when I mentioned that I knew you were chasing me. Now you're telling me that we're going to bed."

She blushed, yet forced herself to meet his eyes. But only for a moment. She had to look away to get a grip on herself. He was right. The level of intensity between them heightened with every look, every touch, and this was neither the time nor the place for it. "The food will get cold," she said quickly. "I'll call the children."

Caleb was still smiling as he watched her rush toward the playground. He couldn't help it. His resolve of the previous night had evaporated the moment he'd seen her and the children at his door.

Fate, opportunity, luck, or chance? Which one of the mysterious elements was governing them? He couldn't guess, but he did know that both he and Cheyenne were acting totally out of character with each other. Normally, he never vacillated in his decisions, but he was doing that now by disregarding his intention not to become involved with her.

His gaze grew thoughtful. Cheyenne had certainly gone against type to chase him. Changes were definitely afoot in Whitneyville.

She returned with Brittany and Jeffrey, and the four of them settled into the booth for lunch, the children sitting together opposite the adults. Boldly, Cheyenne used the opportunity to sit close to Caleb, close enough so that their shoulders touched and their thighs were pressed together.

The children kept up a steady stream of chatter. Cheyenne knew she was smiling and nodding and making the correct responses, but her whole being was focused on Caleb and the intoxicating feelings his nearness evoked in her.

"I didn't know you were coming here!" A child's voice, loud and accusatory, cut into their faux family idyll.

Cheyenne glanced up to see Mollie Harper, Tricia's daughter, standing beside their booth, dangling her Happy Meal by the handles and looking quite cross indeed. Mollie didn't like it when the Merrits had something or went somewhere she didn't, and she was clearly annoyed to discover they'd arrived at her destination before she had.

"We came here first," Jeffrey said smugly. He knew exactly how to wrangle his longtime adversary.

"My daddy brought me," Mollie said, playing her trump card. She always made a point of reminding Brittany and Jeffrey that they were daddyless while she wasn't.

Cheyenne laid her cheeseburger down, her stomach suddenly queasy. She was never very glad to see

Mollie, but running into the child today was particularly onerous. After last night's debacle with Ben Maitland, she was in no hurry to see any of the Harpers.

"Uncle Caleb brought us, and we're going to play with Kimmy who has a hundred Barbies," Brittany said sweetly. "You don't have a hundred Barbies, Mollie."

Ross Harper joined them before Mollie could make a response, but the indignant scowl on her face spoke volumes. "Cheyenne!" Ross was clearly startled to see her—and with a man. "I take it you're feeling better today?"

She smiled weakly. "Yes, thank you, Ross." She took a deep breath. "Ross, I'd like you to meet Caleb Strong. Caleb, this is Ross Harper, my friend Tricia's husband. He owns the Pontiac dealership in Whitneyville."

Having moved to Whitneyville as an adult and not grown up amidst Strong lore, Ross didn't do the usual double take at the name. He also viewed every acquaintance, old and new, as a prospective car buyer, so Cheyenne was not at all surprised when Ross offered Caleb his hand and smiled widely. "Very pleased to meet you, Caleb."

The two men shook hands. "Where's Trish?" Cheyenne asked, bracing herself for the sight of Tricia and her reaction.

"She's at home. She slept late this morning," Ross explained. "You know how she hates to go to bed with a kitchen full of dirty dishes, so she stayed up till almost three cleaning up. The party didn't break up until two o'clock."

Cheyenne looked away. The party. She didn't want to get into that. And she felt guilty, picturing Tricia slaving over dishes at that hour of the night. Should she have stayed and helped with the cleanup? She'd always done so before, but that was after family or neighborhood parties. This was her first "couples only" party at the Harpers' since Evan's death, the first where she'd been paired with a date. Ben Maitland. Her eyes slid to Caleb.

He was talking cars with Ross. New Pontiacs, specifically. Considering how Caleb was dressed, Cheyenne could understand Ross's assumption that Caleb might be in the market for one. It was a mistake he never would have made had Caleb been attired in his usual black biker garb.

The two men parted like old friends. "Be sure to tell Trish we said hi," Caleb called cheerfully.

Ross promised he would and settled himself and Mollie at a nearby table. The girl continued to stare crossly at Brittany and Jeffrey. Finally, Jeffrey stuck his tongue out at her.

"I'm telling!" Mollie's cry of outrage carried across the restaurant. Jeffrey and Brittany slipped under the table, giggling.

"Jeffrey, that was very rude," Cheyenne reproved him.

Caleb reached under the table and patted the children's heads. "Did you know there are two puppy dogs under this table, Cheyenne? Do you think they might be friends of Peppy's?"

Brittany and Jeffrey laughed delightedly and scampered out. "We want more ketchup," Jeffrey announced, and the two raced off to the dispenser. Neither stopped to say hello to Mollie, and she took the opportunity to stick her tongue out at them.

"Not a lot of love lost between Brittany and Jeffrey and the car dealer's kid, hmm?" Caleb said.

"It's so awkward and difficult, and it's getting worse every year," Cheyenne admitted. "Tricia and I have been best friends for years, and our children have detested each other since they were babies." It was the first time she'd ever confided that uncomfortable truth to anyone. But it was so easy to talk to Caleb. She had the feeling she could tell him anything.

Perhaps even the truth about Evan and her not-so-perfect marriage?

"I don't blame the kids for not liking that sour-faced little brat," he said.

"Mollie is very spoiled. But Brittany and Jeffrey do their part to keep the feud going."

Caleb took her hand in his and studied her slim, well-shaped fingers, their nails painted a bright coral. Without thinking, he interlaced her fingers with his own. "Ross will tell your pal Tricia that we were here together. Will she give you an earful about fraternizing with a Strong?"

Would she! Cheyenne thought. He didn't know the half of it. But she was loathe to delve into all of that with him. "I don't lead my life to please Tricia," she said bravely. "If she's really my friend, she'll—she'll understand."

"Understand what? How much you want to go to bed with me?"

Heat swiftly suffused her whole body, and her mind went as blank as a computer screen during a power failure. "I know I should fire off some devastatingly sophisticated comeback," she said weakly, "but I can't think of a single clever thing to say. It's frustrating. I'm an English teacher who has read countless books, and you'd think that would give me an advantage with words. Instead, I'm drawing a complete blank here."

"Good." He laid her hand on his thigh, covering it with his own. "I'm not looking for clever repartee. I want hot unbridled sex, not literary references." He laughed as he said it, but his eyes were glittering with arousal.

Cheyenne looked at her hand, small and white and soft under his. The muscles of his thigh were firm beneath her fingers. It felt as if the very air were electric.

Brittany and Jeffrey returned not a moment too soon. Cheyenne slipped her hand away and purposefully assisted the children with the packets of ketchup. She could feel Caleb's gaze on her, though, and when she stole a glance at him, he grinned rakishly.

"Tonight, Cheyenne?" he asked in a low, low voice, meant for her ears only. She knew what he meant. A jagged sensual thrust pierced her, as unnverving as it was exciting.

She actually wanted to thank Jeffrey when he tried to remove the lid on his milk shake cup and proceeded to spill the entire contents onto the floor. That she could cope with. Caleb Strong was a whole different story.

They arrived at Sallie Strong Kaylor's house a half hour later. If Caleb's younger sister was surprised by her drop-in guests, she gave no evidence of it and welcomed them all warmly. There were several other children there in addition to young Kimmy. They were all as welcoming as Sallie and immediately swept Brittany and Jeffrey upstairs to play.

A toddler clutching a bottle settled himself on Sallie's lap as the adults gathered in the small living room. Seated at one end of the light blue sofa, with Caleb at the other, Cheyenne covertly surveyed the room. It was clean and neat, and the furniture and rug appeared new. She'd already noticed that the exterior of the house was not the dilapidated wreck one might expect to find on this side of the tracks. It was freshly painted, and the roof looked sturdy. In comparison, her house at the stately address of 100 Silver Creek Road was the dilapidated wreck!

Sallie was a plump, pleasant young woman who possessed the characteristic Strong good looks—as well as the disconcerting bluntness. "I remember you from high school," she told Cheyenne with an admiring smile. "You were a senior when I was just a lowly freshman. You seemed sort of like a goddess with lots of beautiful clothes and a gorgeous boyfriend. You were everything. Cheerleader, class officer, Winter Carnival Princess, Homecoming Queen, Prom Queen." Her expression sobered. "I felt terrible when I read in the *Whitneyville Gazette* that your husband had been killed in that car crash in Atlanta. What a tragedy! Things like that shouldn't happen to a Golden Couple like you and Evan Merrit."

Her sympathy and regret seemed genuine, and Cheyenne was oddly tempted to disabuse Sallie of her image of her and Evan. Golden Couple, indeed. She was so tired of living that lie. "Thank you for your kind words, Sallie," she said instead, restraining the peculiar urge to confide the truth. That the Golden Couple would have been in divorce court were it not for the fatal accident. That Evan Merrit had loved another woman, not his wife, the former high school "goddess."

Her eyes connected with Caleb's. He was watching her closely. She stared at him helplessly, knowing she was probably revealing far too much. And not caring.

"That was a long time ago, Sallie," he said. With one swift, smooth movement, he reached for Cheyenne and pulled her closer to him, so close that she was almost sitting on his lap.

Sallie's jaw dropped, and she gaped at them. "I didn't realize—I didn't know—" she stammered. "I thought you were here 'cause of something to do with Joni Lynn, Cheyenne. But you and Caleb . . ." Her voice trailed off, and she gave her head an incredulous shake. "You and Caleb are a couple!" She frowned comically at her brother. "You might've clued me in, Caleb. How long have you two been together?"

Cheyenne looked at Caleb, half-expecting him to say something outrageous, which would probably include a mention of the Magic Carpet Motel. He merely shrugged and said diffidently, "A while."

"Well, I'm thrilled!" Sallie cried. "You know, I always thought you'd be perfect for a woman who already has kids." She turned to Cheyenne, her blue eyes sparkling. "My brother has such a strong sense of family, and he really enjoys children. He'll make a wonderful father and—"

"Sallie!" Even Caleb appeared embarrassed. He made a sound halfway between a groan and a laugh. Cheyenne blushed to the roots of her hair. Caleb might've restrained himself, she thought, but Sallie had picked up the slack in the outrageous remarks department.

Sallie wisely dropped that subject. "Cheyenne, I've never had the chance to thank you for what you've done for Joni Lynn, encouraging her to stay in school—to go to college, even!—and taking her to live with you," she said effusively. "If you hadn't, she probably would've ended up like me and Crystal and too many of our cousins. No high school diploma and a baby at sixteen or seventeen."

Cheyenne conjured up memories of Joni Lynn as a sophomore, a gifted yet indifferent student, more interested in her boyfriend than her studies. But as soon as Cheyenne had begun to tout college as a definite possibility, the girl had dropped her underachieving boyfriend and hit the books.

"I was lucky," Sallie went on. "Things worked out good for me anyway. I married my baby's father and we're happy, but Crystal's life has been a disaster. Dead-end job, a bad marriage and divorce from a no-good louse, a bunch of screwed-up kids by him. Joni Lynn is the only bright spot in Crystal's life, and it would've broken her heart to see her life wrecked too. We're so grateful that you gave Joni Lynn a future to look forward to."

Cheyenne thought of Graham Maitland, Joni Lynn's unacknowledged father. He'd been a brilliant student, winning every academic award Whitneyville High had to offer and going on to excel at the University of Virginia. Graham and Polly's two sons were in the gifted-and-talented program at their respective schools, and had Joni Lynn been raised a Maitland, she would have been tagged for that program in elementary school too. Instead, she'd been labeled a Strong, an irredeemable nothing, and written off. Cheyenne bridled at the unfairness of it all.

"Joni Lynn is bright and talented and determined to succeed," she said softly. "I'm sure she would've been successful without me."

Sallie shook her head. "When you grow up with the kind of loser mentality we did, you need an outsider to step in and prove that they believe in you, that it's really possible for you to be something. Just like that nice old Mr. Mack did for—"

"Sal, I have an idea," Caleb cut in. He took Cheyenne's hand in his and stood up, bringing her to her feet as well. "Since you're already baby-sitting for Cody's and Raina's kids today, how would you feel about keeping Brittany and Jeffrey while—"

"I was going to suggest that myself," Sallie interrupted eagerly. "I know how hard it is to find time alone with kids around all the time. And finding a reliable sitter can be really tough. The most awful thing happened to little Danny here." She nodded at the toddler dozing in her lap. "His mother, our cousin Raina, hired a twelve-year-old from the neighborhood to baby-sit for him. The kid was glued to the TV set when Danny climbed onto a window seat on the second story and somehow unlatched the screen. He fell right out! Thank the Lord their dog was there and broke his fall. Anyway, I told Raina that I'd keep the baby while she's working. I mean, just 'cause a kid turns twelve doesn't mean she's reliable enough to baby-sit."

Cheyenne thought of her own baby-sitter, the previous night, twelve-year-old Darcey Jo Simmons whom Tricia had hired strictly on the basis of her age. Neither of them knew the girl well enough to determine if she was responsible. It suddenly became easy to visualize Darcey Jo watching television while

Jeffrey decided to play Batman and took off from an upper window.

Would pediatrician David Beckworth laugh with the neighbors if Jeffrey had fallen from the second story and landed on Peppy? She thought of the jokes he'd made about the Strongs, about little Danny, that very baby cuddled on Sallie's lap. Remembering all the smug, superior laughter, she felt a stinging, penetrating shame.

Sallie's practical, no-nonsense voice interrupted Cheyenne's chagrined reverie. "You'd better check with your kids and see if they'll stay with me. I won't be insulted if they'd rather go with you. Some kids are shy and don't like to be in a strange place away from home."

That was usually an apt description of Brittany, but not in this case. Cheyenne found her daughter in a room-from-Barbie-heaven, surrounded by too many dolls to count, along with the accompanying toys necessary for their glamorous lifestyle. Brittany, Kimmy, Melanie, and another little girl were playing happily together while Jeffrey and Matthew were occupied with the Nintendo set in another room. Neither Brittany nor Jeffrey had any qualms about staying. Cheyenne had the feeling that getting them to leave, ever, was not going to be easy.

"We'll be back later tonight to pick them up," Caleb said to Sallie as she walked them to Cheyenne's car.

"Sure. Take all the time you want," Sallie said generously. "Are you going into Smithboro for dinner and a movie at that new multiscreen theatre that's opened there?" Clearly that was her idea of a terrific night out.

"Dinner and a movie," Caleb repeated blandly. "Sounds swell, Sal."

"It sounds wonderful," Cheyenne seconded with commendable enthusiasm. "Thank you so much for letting the kids stay, Sallie."

She waved as they drove off.

"I really like your sister," Cheyenne said as Caleb pulled the car into the highway stream of traffic. "She's so warm and friendly. She made me feel like I've known her for ages."

"Sallie's a longtime fan of yours, dating way back to the bad old days at Whitneyville High. It's funny the way younger kids look up to older ones, how high school freshmen view the seniors as celebrities of unattainable glamour and then remember them down through the years. Like Sallie with you." He paused. "And you with Penny Sherwood."

Cheyenne made a choking sound, but before she could protest his outlandish supposition, he was talking again.

"Penny Sherwood . . . An interesting choice of idol, Cheyenne. Certainly a revealing one. While my little sister Sallie wanted to be you, the embodiment of the Popular Teen Princess, *you* wanted to be Penny—hot, sexy, impulsive."

"You couldn't be more wrong!" she exclaimed. "I didn't admire Penny Sherwood, I was appalled by her!"

"Oh, yeah? And you wouldn't have traded your Prom Queen tiara for just one passionate late-night session in the backseat of a car down at the grove with me?"

Cheyenne drew in a sharp, ragged breath. Caleb was laughing. Kidding with her. His retrofantasy shouldn't have the power to affect her, to make her blood run hot in her veins, to make her skin flushed and feverish. Images of herself and Caleb, kissing, touching, necking, petting, flashed before her mind's eye, shifting in kaleidoscopic fashion. An intensely pleasurable knife-like thrust in her groin almost made her gasp aloud.

It was definitely time for a reality check. "I was too young and too scared and too conventional back then," she said in a husky voice she hardly recognized as her own. "I couldn't have handled you."

"You're still young and scared and conventional," he countered.

"That's not true. I'm different now."

"Hmm, on second thought, maybe you are. You climb on the back of a motorcycle late at night, you make out with the town hood, you even chase after him, showing up at the Magic Carpet Motel in tight jeans and wiggling your cute little butt." He knocked his forehead with his palm, feigning shock. "Good Lord, you've *become* Penny Sherwood!"

She laughed. "You're crazy."

"And you're not a scared, uptight little girl anymore. Think you can handle me now, Miss Cheyenne?"

Nine

They stopped at a red light, and Caleb looked at her with hungry eyes, so vibrantly male that every feminine instinct Cheyenne possessed responded. Her laughter abruptly ended. A sharp and urgent yearning burned inside her, taking over and making coherent thought impossible. She squirmed in her seat, crossing her legs to try to ease the swelling ache between them.

He reached over and laid his hand on top of hers. The warm, heavy weight of that hand on her lap was an added stimulation to her already overloaded senses. "Caleb," she whispered, hearing the plea in her voice, yet unable to articulate the terrible need coursing through her.

The light turned green then, and Caleb replaced both his hands on the wheel and drove through the intersection. Cheyenne's insides knotted with frustration. How could something as stupidly mundane as a traffic signal intrude on one of the most intense moments of her life?

"It's only two-thirty," he said with a nonchalance she envied. "We've got a while until dinner."

"Yes." She twisted the shoulder strap of her purse. She felt dizzy. Her whole body throbbed with desire.

"What do you want to do until then?"

The conversation struck her as surreal. They were definitely talking on two levels, but she couldn't find the courage to bluntly state the obvious. "Well, we could go shopping, I suppose," she heard herself say in her most socially polite voice. She winced. Any aspirations she might have harbored toward Penny Sherwoodism had been dealt a severe blow with that inane suggestion.

"Shopping in downtown Whitneyville," he said dryly. "Okay, if that's what you want, that's what we'll do."

She stared blindly ahead. "Probably the last thing I want is to go shopping in downtown Whitneyville," she whispered.

"What do you want most, Cheyenne?"

"You're not going to make this easy, are you?" She gulped. "You're going to make me say it."

"Yes," he said, his voice low and raspy. "And not because I want to humiliate you or establish a defense or play word games as a strategy for seduction. What I want is a woman who is willing and honest and not afraid to admit that she wants me."

Her heart was pounding violently. Around her, everything began to blur and swirl. Could she do it? Did she dare tell him that she wanted him desperately? That she hadn't known such incredible desire existed, and never would have if he hadn't come into her life? That whoever he was and whatever he did, she wanted to be with him all the time, wherever he happened to be?

"Caleb, I—" She had to stop to breathe. Her mouth was dry, her pulses speeding. "I'm in love with you."

For a long, silent moment the words seemed to hang suspended between them. She was stunned by her own revelation. When she dared to slant a quick look at him, she saw that his mouth was set in a grim, taut line.

"I—I guess I'm hopeless at this," she said, her voice

wavering. She tried to smile but could manage only a sad little twist of her lips. "I was supposed to say that I want to go to bed with you and instead, I tell you that I love you."

He sighed. "It's not unusual for a woman to confuse sexual desire with love, Cheyenne. You want to go to bed with me and you can't justify that unless you redefine your feelings as love."

"You sound like a magazine article," she said indignantly. Having her spontaneous declaration of love so objectively dissected was mortifying in the extreme. She was suddenly furious with him. "Or are you speaking from your vast personal experience? It must be tough, having to cope with all those women who've lusted after you and then convinced themselves that they'd fallen in love with you. Poor Caleb. And now, here I am, complicating your life even further by telling you that I love you when we haven't even made it back to the Magic Carpet Motel!"

Caleb stifled a groan. This wasn't working out quite the way he had hoped. Well, he'd been in sticky situations before and he knew how to extricate himself from them. To get out of this one, all he had to do was back off. He'd dispassionately explain that they were at cross purposes, turn the car around, and pick up the children at Sallie's. He'd take them all home and then stay away from them. Cheyenne would not come after him again, not after a scene like this. That was a given. He would be free.

Or would he? Had he ever really been free? His past and his feelings toward this town and his family hardly made for a feckless, carefree existence. Did he go looking for complications and obligations? A relationship with a widow and two small children certainly wasn't as easy and convenient as one with an unencumbered single woman with an uncomplicated past. Yet none of those relationships had engaged him at all, while Cheyenne already had a hold on him that seemed alarmingly unshakable.

"Cheyenne, I just want you to be aware of the risk you'll be taking." He began to perspire as he realized he didn't sound at all dispassionate. The opposite, in fact. "After . . . uh . . . um, sex, it—things will be even more emotional and complex. You'll feel vulnerable and attached and open. You'll feel romantic and close to me. . . ."

He paused and gulped for breath. He was in trouble. Since when did he mumble and stumble over the word sex? Furthermore, he found himself wanting her to feel all those things he was warning her against! Instead of extricating himself, he was sinking in deeper.

"Oh, you don't have to worry about me having those kinds of feelings afterward," Cheyenne said with a nervous little laugh, then she took a deep breath. For better or for worse, she was going to tell him the truth. She just couldn't pretend anymore.

"Evan and I rarely made love after our first year of marriage. Whenever we did, I certainly didn't feel close to him afterward. I felt disappointed and embarrassed and more alone than I'd ever felt in my life. In fact, thinking back on it makes me realize what a terrible mistake I'd be making if I went to bed with you."

She pictured herself lying beside Caleb, feeling alienated and desolate, fighting back tears of despair. Instinctively she knew it would be much worse failing with Caleb than it had ever been with Evan.

"Sex just isn't for me." She shivered. "I think you'd better take me home, Caleb." The excitement, the sexual tension had dissolved, leaving her depressed and feeling as flat as an open can of day-old soda pop. "I'll let Brittany and Jeffrey play at Sallie's awhile longer and pick them up around five. I'm sure she'll—"

"So Golden Boy Merrit was lousy in bed, huh?" Caleb interrupted. "That figures."

"It wasn't him, it was me," she said wearily. "He had

a girlfriend who told me what a wonderful lover he was. Their—Their love life was ideal."

"What?"

She nodded, determined to tell him everything. "The woman's name was Mindy. She came to see me the day after Evan was killed. She was in the throes of grief, and the whole story came tumbling out. He'd been with her that night and was driving back to Whiteneyville when a truck hit his car head-on. They'd met when I was pregnant with Brittany and had been having an affair ever since. According to Mindy, Evan considered Jeffrey an unplanned accident. He intended to divorce me when the baby was a year old and then marry her. He was upset about having to wait that long, but he was concerned about . . . gossip."

"Like it's perfectly okay to dump your wife when your kids are one and two years old," Caleb said sardonically. "Hell, they're practically on their own at those advanced ages. Merrit was a bastard, Cheyenne."

"He was wildly in love for the first time in his life," she said quietly. Had Evan experienced these same compelling, passionate feelings for Mindy that she felt for Caleb? For the first time, she was beginning to understand—and maybe even forgive.

"Mindy had lots of pictures and letters, and she showed them to me that day," she continued softly. "It was so strange. Evan and I had dated all those years, we were married and had two babies, but I never saw him look as happy as he did in those pictures with her. And he never said or wrote the things to me that he did to her. It's sad, isn't it? He was stuck with me all that time. We never even made love until our wedding night, and it was a complete flop. Then, when he finally fell in love, he—he died."

"Oh, jeez." Caleb pulled the car into the parking lot behind Hinton's Pharmacy and braked to a stop. "And ever since, you've been playing the role of the bereaved widow. Letting Evan Merrit keep his tragic image of the golden-boy-who-died-too-young."

She managed a ghostly smile. "For Brittany and Jeffrey's sake, I hope the truth never comes out. The official story is that he was in Atlanta on business. Incredibly enough, it's another secret that's somehow been kept from the town grapevine."

"And you've been blaming yourself for the lousy sex in your marriage. Believing that you deserved to have your husband cheat on you. You're convinced that you're no good in bed, that it's all your fault that Hot Pants Merrit found himself a piece on the side and got himself killed getting it." Caleb shook his head. "Damn, you come with a lot of emotional baggage, sweetheart."

"Yes." She managed to conceal it well, as long as no one got too close. Caleb had done that without even trying.

He opened the car door. "I need to pick up a couple of things in the drugstore. You can wait here or come in with me."

"I'll wait here." Her confession left her feeling drained. She rolled down the window and leaned her head against the back of the seat as the car door closed after him. A pleasant breeze drifted into the car.

Having revealed everything to him, she waited, expecting to feel stupid or ashamed or both. Oddly enough, she didn't. Instead, she felt a peculiar relief to have voiced the truth at last. To have, just this once, escaped from the long, painful lie she'd been living.

She didn't realize the car parked next to her belonged to Graham and Polly Maitland until she saw them walking toward her. The urge to dive down on the floor was almost irresistible, but she forced herself to remain seated as the Maitlands approached. She waved politely to them.

"I hope you're feeling better today, Cheyenne," Polly

said. Though a dozen years older, she'd always been friendly to Cheyenne, treating her as a peer. But today Cheyenne noticed that the smile didn't reach Polly's eyes. Clearly, Ben had made some pernicious remarks about her when he'd returned to the Harpers'.

"I am, thank you," she replied, dutifully matching Polly's propriety.

Graham Maitland said nothing, but his face was pinched and ashen, his mouth frozen into a twisted grimace. His eyes briefly met Cheyenne's, then he looked away. A flash of insight struck her. *He knows that I know the truth about Joni Lynn.* And by his sickly, anxious demeanor, he was obviously terrified by what she might do with the knowledge.

Cheyenne was suddenly filled with an overwhelming contempt for him. For the past year Graham's daughter had lived just two blocks away from him and he'd never once displayed the slightest interest in her. He had never bothered to ask about her or stop over to see the girl, not even on some drummed-up pretext. And all those years before, knowing where his child was living and how, he had never contributed any badly needed support for her, had never even inquired about her welfare.

And why not? Because all that mattered to Graham Maitland was his status in the town and keeping the Maitland name gossip-free—even though neither of those concerns had prevented him from fathering a child with Crystal Strong seventeen years ago.

Cheyenne promised herself then and there that she was no longer going to live her life by the dictates of the town.

Polly made a few innocuous remarks about the weather and the smaller-than-usual crowds in the stores that day. "More and more people are driving out to that mall beyond Smithboro to shop. When the new Dix-Mart opens here, we can kiss downtown Whitneyville good-bye. Except for the bank, of course," she added with a satisfied smile. "We'll be thriving, thanks to Dix-Mart."

Graham turned suddenly and concentrated on fitting the car key into the lock. "We've got to go, Polly," he said tersely. "Immediately."

Cheyenne glanced over to see Caleb striding toward the car, a paper bag in his hands. Almost frantically, Graham flung open his car door. He was trying to run away from Caleb, Cheyenne realized. But it was too late. Caleb had already reached her car.

"Good afternoon, Graham, Polly," he said. Cheyenne wondered how he could make the greeting sound positively chilling. His smile also showed a gift for menace.

Graham nodded nervously. Polly's nod was cool and perfunctory. Neither spoke, but climbed silently into their car. Caleb slid behind the wheel of Cheyenne's car and started the motor. The Maitlands were watching, but Cheyenne didn't care. She would rather be with Caleb Strong than a worm like Graham Maitland any day of the week.

"Ah, small towns," Caleb remarked drolly as he pulled out of the parking lot. "You're always running into folks you know."

"Graham tried to get away before you saw him," Cheyenne said. "I think he's afraid of you."

Caleb smiled slowly. "He's right to be." He dropped the paper bag into her lap. "This is for you."

Surprised, she looked inside. There was a two-pound box of candy—milk chocolates, assorted nuts, and creams. And a box of condoms. Her heart took off like a runaway train.

She quickly closed the bag. She was speechless.

"I didn't know what kind of candy you like," he said. "So I bought the assortment. I chose . . . the other based on my own personal preferences. I can exchange them if you prefer another brand."

"If you're trying to shock me, you've succeeded

beyond your wildest expectations," she murmured, crinkling the bag with nervous fingers.

"I've gotten past the stage where I optimistically carry a condom around in my wallet, hoping I might get lucky," he said dryly. His expression grew serious. "And I've seen my own sisters end up pregnant because passion obliterated precautions. I made a promise to myself years ago that I'd never do that to a woman and I never have. This stop and this purchase were necessary, Cheyenne."

She cleared her throat. "I . . . um, I thought we'd decided to call this—this whole thing off."

"I guess you were mistaken, weren't you?"

He drove through Whitneyville's business district and headed south, to the exclusive Silver Creek neighborhood. Cheyenne sat silently beside him, clutching the bag. She no longer felt weary and emotionally drained. She could feel every nerve ending coming vitally alive. She was in love, and the man she loved was about to become her lover.

Caleb pulled the car into her garage and took her hand as they walked into the house. Once inside, he picked her up in his arms and carried her up the stairs. She was still holding on to the paper bag.

He walked down the hall, glancing into the bedrooms they passed. There was Brittany's pink-and-white little girl's room with the ruffled curtains and Victorian dollhouse. Jeffrey's, done in primary colors with his red-and-blue bed in the shape of a race car. Joni Lynn's, with posters of rock stars taped onto the walls.

Cheyenne's bedroom was at the end of the hall. It was a completely feminine room, done in soft shades of rose and ivory. She had hastily redecorated it herself a few weeks after Evan was killed. She hadn't wanted any traces of him or reminders of his betrayal in what was now her room alone.

A bolt of caution and fear struck her at the thought of Evan. Given her track record in the bedroom, she was taking an awful risk. And Caleb had offered her no words of love or commitment. There was nothing to keep him from walking out the door and never returning. An odd lump formed in her throat. The thought of his rejection was terrible to contemplate.

She knew, though, that she would never ask him for words that he didn't mean. She'd already gone that route, listening to Evan promise to "love, honor, and cherish" her in front of a crowded church. He had done none of those things, and she had learned the hard way that words were easy to say and just as easily discounted. No, she would not demand a declaration of anything from Caleb Strong.

He set her on her feet beside the bed and gazed down at her, his eyes penetrating. He seemed to be looking into her, reading her mind. "Forget Merrit," he said firmly. "What happened between the two of you has nothing to do with you and me."

Her startled expression confirmed to him that she'd been apprehensively reminiscing about her late husband. Caleb was a little surprised himself at how closely attuned he was to her. And that he'd wanted to offer her the comfort and reassurance she needed.

"Merrit's ghost isn't going to come between us," he promised. "I won't let you confuse me with him."

He cupped her shoulders and began to knead the taut muscles of her back with his long, strong fingers. Cheyenne stared down at the rose-colored rug as a sensual languor began to seep through her body. "I'm nervous," she admitted.

"I know, baby." He kept up his sensuous massage, his hands gliding lower. "I know."

She breathed a soft sigh, but moments later she was back on guard again. It was such a risk, such a risk. Yet she was in love with him and she wanted him in the most profound, elemental way. Never had she felt so conflicted.

"Suppose I told you that I don't want to do this,"

she heard herself say in a voice that sounded strangely far away. "Would you let me go?"

"Of course. If that's what you wanted, Cheyenne." But he spoke in the smooth, confident tones of a man who was very sure of himself and his sexual power. He was willing to let her go because he knew she wouldn't leave him.

He pulled her against him and began to nibble on her neck. "Do you want me to let you go, Cheyenne?"

She could feel him hard and urgent against her. Shivering, she pressed into him. Her eyes were half-closed, and her lips parted softly. "No," she said huskily. "Caleb, I want you so much."

It was surprisingly easy to confess. Liberating too. Slowly, then with increasing confidence, she touched his mouth, her fingers tracing its firm, sensual shape. She lifted her face to his, and the passion burning in his fiery eyes made her feel feminine and irresistible, as if she were the sexiest, most desirable woman in the world. It was a heady feeling for a woman whose sexual confidence had been crushed, and she loved him all the more for restoring it.

The way she was looking at him . . . the way she was touching him . . . Caleb rarely felt his head spin, but it was spinning now. The spasm of desire that seized him was so sharp, he could hardly stand. Keeping his arms wrapped around her, he sank to the bed, taking her with him.

Their gazes locked. For a long moment, they lay together. Words seemed unnecessary, but he gave them to her anyway. Sexy words that teased and tempted and tantalized. Tender words that aroused and soothed and melted away all and any inhibitions.

Cheyenne was achingly aware of the erotic changes taking place in her body. Her breasts felt full and swollen and exquisitely sensitive as they pressed against his hard chest. Deep inside her was a sweet, aching hunger that grew and built in strength and force, until she could no longer lie still under his caressing hands.

He slipped his leg between hers, sliding his thigh back and forth against the throbbing, most vibrantly female part of her body. A deep, radiating pleasure rocketed through her as he began a gentle, rocking motion. She moaned and moved with him, for him, in an excruciatingly passionate simulation.

Her volatile response triggered a wild thrill that reverberated through him. "You're so sexy, so beautiful," he said hoarsely. "I've never wanted a woman as much as I want you, Cheyenne."

Joy burst within her. She believed him. That she, Cheyenne Whitney Merrit, former repressed good girl, former rejected wife, could inspire such arousal in a man like Caleb Strong, who was the embodiment of every woman's fantasy of the virile male . . . why, it was *her* fantasy come true!

Enraptured, she cupped his face with her hands and touched her lips to his. His reaction was quick as lightning. His mouth opened over hers, and he rolled on top of her, letting her body absorb the full, warm weight of him.

Their kiss was hard and hot and sexy. And not nearly enough for either of them. His hands found her breasts, and he massaged them in the same primal rhythm of his tongue's movements in her mouth. A tidal wave of desire, of need, crashed through her, and suddenly for the first time in her life, she became sexually aggressive, pulling his shirt from the waistband of his slacks, sliding her hands under it to feel the smooth warmth of his skin.

She explored the wiry-soft mat of hair on his chest, luxuriously running her fingers through it. She found his taut nipples and learned their shape. She couldn't keep her hands off him. The wild, compulsive need to touch him was too powerful. "You feel so good," she breathed when he lifted his mouth from hers.

He sat up, and she raised herself to sit beside him. He smiled into her eyes. "Baby, you ain't felt nothin' yet," he teased, lapsing into drawling slang.

"As an English teacher, I feel compelled to correct your grammar." Her eyes gleamed. "Repeat after me, 'Baby, you haven't felt anything yet.'"

"Haven't I?" His deft fingers had her blouse unbuttoned within seconds. "Hmm, I'll have to rectify that."

He slid the blouse from her shoulders, then drank in the sight of her softly rounded breasts, which voluptuously filled the cups of her lacy white bra. He was surprised to feel his fingers trembling with anticipation as he unclasped the front fastener of the bra.

"It's been a long, long time since unfastening a bra was a major thrill for me," he muttered between shallow breaths. He watched her shrug the lacy garment off, his eyes riveted to her desire-swollen breasts. "But with you . . . everything feels brand-new, Cheyenne."

His admission thrilled her, and she smiled with love and passion as she reached for him. She'd never undressed a man before, but she disposed of his shirt with astonishing dexterity. When her fingers lowered to the buckle of his belt, though, he caught her hand and carried it to his mouth, halting her.

"We're going to take it slow this time," he said huskily, lowering her back down on the mattress. His mouth moved to her breast, further sensitizing it with soft, gentle kisses, until she moaned and arched up to him, offering herself. His lips closed over one taut pink peak. She felt his touch deep inside her womb, and when he began to suck, she cried out as her inner muscles clenched and spasmed with a madly pleasurable ache that demanded to be assuaged.

In a haze of passion, she felt him unzip her jeans and slide them down her legs. His mouth lowered to her stomach, the tip of his tongue probing her navel.

She whimpered, tossing her head back and forth, as the yearning inside her grew so forceful, she raised her hips to him in a silent plea for release.

He kissed her through her white bikini panties, and his breath, heated and moist, filtered through the fabric, making her wetter, hotter. Suddenly even that flimsy barrier was intolerable to them both. Swiftly, he skimmed her panties from her body, baring her to him.

"Cheyenne. Baby. Cheyenne," he chanted, too incoherent with desire to be able to say anything else. He was consumed and driven by his passion for her. He'd intended to take her slowly and gently, but his gentlemanly intentions were obliterated by his shocking loss of control.

He had to be inside her, to sink into her moist feminine heat and feel her womanly softness surround him. Frantically, he shucked off the rest of his clothes.

Cheyenne stared at his naked body through passion-hazed eyes. He was exceedingly well built and superbly muscled. Everywhere. He was strong and powerful and thoroughly masculine, and she wanted to know everything there was to know about him. To learn the contours and textures of his body, to experience his taste and his scent. She reached for him, opening her arms and her legs to him.

Caleb's long fingers tangled in the luxuriant pale curls shielding her womanhood. He deftly parted the satiny folds, easing his finger inside her to test her readiness. "Oh yes, baby," he murmured as he felt her heat and her wetness. Her soft flesh clenched reflexively around his finger.

It was an effort to leave her, even for a second, but he did so to reach for the precautionary packet in the bag on the nightstand. He would never hurt her by not protecting her. "Cheyenne, I can't wait any longer," he said thickly.

She didn't want him to wait. Intense spirals of heat

were uncoiling deep within her as her body melted and flowed, readying itself to him. "Now, Caleb, please," she whispered, clinging to him. "Love me now."

He surged into her with one deliciously slow, strong stroke. He filled her completely, and she shuddered, lost in a wild torrent of sensations. He began to move within her, possessing her with deep, hard thrusts. The pleasure was so intense, so sharp and swift, it was almost unbearable.

Instinctively, she wrapped her legs around him, moving in a counterpoint rhythm. She'd never known it could be like this, that she would ever feel this way, wanting more and more of him. Deeper, harder. Again and again and again, until she was completely lost in the explosive, rapturous tension that kept building and building . . . And suddenly sent her spinning out of herself in a timeless moment of sheer, raw ecstasy.

Caleb heard her soft cries as she convulsed around him. Her abandon hurled him over the edge. Inside her, his hard-driving heat exploded into a roaring inferno, consuming them both as they gave in to the intense, searing pleasure.

Ten

Cheyenne hovered between sleep and wakefulness, her mind drifting, her body relaxed and languid as she lay, tucked spoon-fashion, in the curve of Caleb's body. She was sublimely conscious of the feel of him against her, his wiry chest hair tickling her back, his hard thighs entwined with hers. His arms were around her, holding her possessively, and she felt protected and cherished. And happier than she'd ever been in her entire life. She closed her eyes and sighed blissfully.

"It's almost six." His voice punctured her dreamy fugue state. He nuzzled her neck and worried the lobe of her ear with his teeth. "Did you want to go into Smithboro for dinner and then catch a movie?"

She groaned a protest. "I don't want to move!"

"Very good." He laughed softly. His fingers were lightly caressing the slight swell of her belly. "A few hours ago, you'd have uttered something politely idiotic, like when you suggested shopping when you were desperate to jump into the sack with me. I'm glad a few hours in my bed has cured you of—"

"This is *my* bed, and you're an overconfident snake!" she interrupted, trying her best to sound sternly indignant. She didn't quite succeed. A playful grin kept threatening to break through. "It would serve you right if I were to say, 'Dinner and a movie? Such a lovely way to spend an evening,'" She used her most synthetically charming voice.

His fingers slipped lower, finding her pliant and ready for him. "I taught you some new words today," he murmured against her ear. "Let me hear you use them."

His thumb caressed her, sending starbursts of pleasure exploding through her. Breathlessly, Cheyenne arched against him. She used her newfound physical and verbal knowledge to catapult them both into glorious, shattering intimacy.

An hour later they were sitting at the kitchen table, eating cold sliced ham, potato salad, and coleslaw, leftovers Cheyenne had retrieved from the refrigerator. She supplemented the meal with sliced tomatoes from the garden and the previous day's corn bread and apple cake.

"This is great," Caleb said with pleasure. "Your leftovers are better than what used to pass for Thanksgiving dinner at our house."

Cheyenne laughed. "I don't believe your mother was as bad a cook as you claim." She felt giddy and high as a kite, floating on a bubble of supreme joy.

"Believe it, honey." He heaped his plate with more food. For the first time in his life, that old adage about the way to a man's heart being through his stomach made sense to him. He let himself imagine coming home to meals like this every night. No more plastic food out of cardboard boxes and cans. No more drive-thru-window cuisine.

He looked across the table at Cheyenne, who was gazing at him, her eyes shining with love. She had looked at him that way when they'd lain in bed together, flushed and replete from the best sex he'd ever had. He felt his body stir. After spending the afternoon in bed, it seemed impossible that he could want her again so soon.

But he did. She was so sexy, so passionate, yet so loving and sweet. He'd never encountered such a potent combination, in or out of bed. And though she had expressed her feelings for him without reservation, though she had surrendered to him completely, generously giving him everything, she had not asked that he reciprocate in kind. In fact, she had made no emotional demands on him whatsoever.

That puzzled him. There had been a few times when he'd been totally vulnerable, completely at the mercy of the emotions roiling within him, but she hadn't pressed her advantage. She hadn't asked him personal questions about his life or his job, she hadn't demanded any sort of commitment.

And he found himself wanting to give her . . . *something.* He considered telling her about his executive position with Dix-Mart, filling in those missing fourteen years that she still knew nothing about. But he held back. Did he find the idea that she loved the outcast that he used to be, that the town still thought him to be, too enthralling to give up?

He was under no illusions that if he were to reveal the truth about his present circumstances, he would suddenly be considered as eligible in Whitneyville as he was in Mobile. There wasn't a single door that the combination of money, power, and success wouldn't open. Everybody loved a winner, and to the world outside of Whitneyville, Caleb W. Strong was indeed a winner.

But it was Caleb Strong, loser, whom Cheyenne thought she'd gone to bed with. She didn't even know the winner existed. He felt a fierce tenderness for her, a powerful and passionate force that swept through him, galvanizing him to action.

He reached across the table and covered her hand with his. Their fingers seemed to interlock automatically. "Cheyenne," he began, not sure what he was going to say.

Would he have told her everything if the kitchen door hadn't swung open at that very moment? He didn't know, but the point was moot anyway, for Joni Lynn and Peppy rushed inside. The dog ran to his dish and began to gulp the bits of ham Cheyenne had placed there for him. Joni Lynn came to a screeching halt and stared at the couple holding hands at the table.

"Wow!" she gasped. "Is this what it looks like? Or something else entirely?"

Cheyenne withdrew her hand from Caleb's and nervously adjusted the lapels of her pink chenille robe. She was well aware of the picture she and Caleb presented—she in her robe with her hair tousled and not a trace of makeup on, Caleb wearing only his trousers, his hair sexily mussed. There must be words to use upon such an occasion, but for the life of her, she couldn't think of a single one.

Caleb had no such problems. "I guess it depends on what it looks like," he drawled laconically.

Grandmother Whitney's clock on the mantel in the living room chimed eight, and Cheyenne hopped to her feet, flushed and flustered. "Oh my goodness, I have to pick up Brittany and Jeffrey. By the time I get them home and ready for bed, it'll be long past their bedtime."

"Where are the kids?" Joni Lynn asked interestedly.

"At Sallie's," Caleb said. He stood up too. "They've been there most of the day. Joni Lynn, could we prevail upon you for a favor?"

Joni Lynn smiled. "If it happens to be taking Cheyenne's car to pick up Brittany and Jeffrey at Aunt Sallie's, the answer is yes."

"The kid is psychic," Caleb said dryly.

"You don't have to be psychic to know that you two

want to be alone," Joni Lynn shot back, grinning at the pair. She left the kitchen, humming to herself.

As soon as they heard the front door bang shut, Caleb pulled Cheyenne into his arms. "We have enough time for a few long, slow good-night kisses before the troops arrive. Let's take advantage of it." His lips touched hers while he was talking, and he punctuated each word with a short, staccato kiss. "Starting right now."

They were both fully dressed when Joni Lynn returned with Brittany and Jeffrey less than a half hour later.

"Mommy, Mommy, we had so much fun!" Brittany exclaimed, flinging her arms around her mother. Caleb was the next to receive an effervescent hug from her. "Kimmy is my new best friend! And Aunt Sallie said I could come over to play tomorrow!"

"We ate dinner at Aunt Sallie's too," Jeffrey put in. "We had SpaghettiOs right out of the can. I never tasted anything so good!"

Caleb gave a yelp of laughter. "Uh-oh. I think we have a Strong changeling in our midst." He scooped up both children, one under each arm, and carried them, squealing with laughter, upstairs. Cheyenne was right on his heels. "Joni Lynn is going to help you with your bath and tuck you into bed," he went on, "while your mom drives me back to the Magic Carpet Motel."

He had already decided that he wasn't ready to say good night to Cheyenne just yet, despite the proliferation of good-night kisses they'd exchanged. "Is that okay with you two?"

Both children nodded their approval. "Is the Magic Carpet Motel the place with the red and purple doors?" Brittany asked.

"Why don't you live here?" Jeffrey offered. "We have lots of rooms. Not red doors and purple doors, though," he added thoughtfully, as if considering the appeal of those gaudy doors.

"No more dawdling," Cheyenne said quickly, turning on the taps. A rush of water cascaded into the tub. "It's getting late and—"

"I'll take over," Joni Lynn said, her eyes gleaming. "You drive Uncle Caleb back to the Magic Carpet, Cheyenne." She grinned, clearly pleased to be included in the machinations of adult romance. "I won't wait up for you."

Cheyenne flushed scarlet. "Oh, I—I'll be right back."

"No, you won't." Caleb locked a possessive arm around her waist and hauled her against him. "Don't wait up, Joni Lynn."

The motel room was so dark that Cheyenne couldn't see even a glimmer of light, as Caleb closed the door behind them. Then she was in his arms and he was kissing her, and her heart was pumping pure liquid fire through her body. They fell to the bed without breaking the passionate kiss, and tore at each other's clothes with a wild urgency enhanced by the total darkness.

Being unable to see, only to feel and to touch, was potently erotic. Caleb's mouth and hands pleasured her in the dark. She didn't know where or what he would do next. Each caress was an exciting sensual shock. In her mind's eye, she visualized the rip-cord muscles of his body, which she examined so thoroughly that afternoon in her sun-drenched bedroom. Dizzy with arousal, she stroked her hands over him, testing her own powers while surrendering to his demands.

They had spent the day learning how to arouse each other to white-hot readiness, and the lessons were put to good use. Their bodies merged, fast and hard, and their moans and sighs filled the blackness as her dark warmth sealed around him. Their climax was swift and mutual, tumultuous and exquisitely satisfying. For a long time afterward, they lay in the darkness, tangled in each other's arms, silent and serene.

"I'll follow you into town on my bike," Caleb said, kissing her one last time before bundling her into her car. He felt protective and possessive. It seemed insane to send her out alone into the night when she could be safely asleep in his arms, in his bed. But he couldn't argue with her reluctance to leave Joni Lynn and the children alone all night. He understood and approved of her sense of maternal responsibility.

Things were getting very complicated, very fast, though. It was probably time for him to make the decision again not to become involved with Cheyenne. He'd made it at least a dozen times since they'd remet. He'd also discovered—at least a dozen times—that though the decision was easy to make, it was considerably more difficult to implement.

He gazed down into her love-flushed face. Her lips were swollen from his kisses, her hazel eyes were luminous. This time he didn't bother to make the decision not to see her again. He recognized an exercise in futility when he faced one.

Cheyenne nuzzled her face against his bare chest. The cotton shirt he'd thrown on was unbuttoned, and she took full advantage of that fact. "Will you call me tomorrow?" she asked softly, ignoring a lifetime of rules in strategy and propriety between males and females. Rule number one was Never Try To Nail Down That Phone Call. But she was too involved, too committed, too much in love to play by the rules of the game. Even if he wasn't.

"I'll call," he replied, easing her behind the wheel of her car. His stomach contracted with a peculiar ache. She'd been out of his arms for mere seconds, and he was missing her already. "What time?"

"We go to church at eleven and are usually home within an hour. Do you want to come over for lunch?"

He had the strongest impulse to join them for church. He fought it, just as determinedly. *He was not going to go gaga over this woman!* Although he sometimes did attend services in Mobile, he wasn't about to stun the godly parishioners of Whitneyville by appearing in church with Cheyenne and her brood. "Okay. Lunch," he agreed. "I'll be there around noon." He headed toward his bike.

"Caleb?" Her voice halted him, and he turned around to see her gazing adoringly at him. "I just wanted to thank you," she said, her voice painfully earnest. "This has been the best day—and night—of my life."

His heart started to pound so erratically, he could hardly breathe. A searing sensation ripped through him, and his tongue suddenly felt thick and awkward, making it difficult to talk. "For Pete's sakes, Cheyenne," he muttered. "Don't say things like that."

Cheyenne nodded and smiled a little wistfully. She understood his unease; he wasn't in love with her, and such statements pressured him.

She drove carefully back to Silver Creek Road, watching Caleb on his motorcycle through the rear-view mirror. When she pulled into her driveway, he turned around in the street and rode off, giving a farewell wave. Inexplicably, tears filled her eyes.

She would see him tomorrow, she reminded herself. She must not think beyond that. She would take things as they came, day to day, and not waste time worrying and wondering about a future that might never happen. She'd already lived that folly, and she was certainly smart enough not to repeat her same old mistakes.

But was she about to make a whole set of new mistakes? Cheyenne pushed the haunting question from her mind.

The next morning Caleb was waiting on the front porch when the four of them returned from church.

He found himself smiling at the sight of them, all dressed in their Sunday best, talking and laughing as they walked from the car to the front door. Brittany and Jeffrey, affectionate as always, ran to him and hugged him joyfully. Joni Lynn gave him a niecely peck on the cheek.

Cheyenne hung back, watching him with the others, her cheeks flushed, her eyes bright. A tremulous smile teased the corners of her mouth. She wanted to throw her arms around him, but the children's presence inhibited her.

Caleb's eyes met and held hers. He wanted to pull her into his arms, but restrained the impulse. After all, there were children present. "Who wants to go on a picnic?" he asked those children, while still gazing at their mother.

"Me! Me! Me!" chorused Brittany and Jeffrey.

"I'd love to, but I have too much homework, Uncle Caleb," Joni Lynn said apologetically. "I have a French quiz and a math quiz tomorrow, and I have to write a fourteen-line sonnet in iambic pentameter for Honors English."

"Write a sonnet in iambic pentameter? Now there's a useful skill for today's job market," he said dryly.

"Be careful what you say, there's an English teacher present," Cheyenne warned. She hadn't been aware that she'd been in motion, but somehow, she was now standing next to him.

Her nearness dissolved Caleb's restraint. "And what are you going to do in retaliation, English teacher?" He pulled her back against him, wrapping his arms around her waist and nuzzling her neck, right in front of his niece and Cheyenne's children. All three regarded the couple with avid interest.

Cheyenne didn't care. It was so good to be back in his arms. She melted against him, placing her hands over his. "I just might make you read a book of sonnets aloud and then have you critique each one."

"Kinky," he whispered in her ear.

They both laughed and then moved apart. But the momentary constraint and awkwardness between them was broken, never to recur. Not during their afternoon picnic at Piney Creek, not during the next weeks in which they saw each other nearly every day, or the weekends they spent together in Atlanta, twice with the children, the others alone while the kids stayed with his sister Sallie.

In the city, she saw another side of him entirely. His tastes, his manners, and dress were sophisticated and extended far beyond small town Whitneyville. One unforgettable Saturday in Atlanta, he took her shopping and bought her a stunning white beaded dress, a gorgeous one-of-a-kind creation that managed to be both tasteful and sexy. She wore it that night to dinner at an exclusive restaurant in one of the city's historic homes, then to the theater for the opening night of a much-heralded show.

Caleb was as much at home in that environment as he was watching a Clint Eastwood movie and dining at the local Dairy Queen back home. She had many, many questions, but she didn't ask them. When he was ready to tell her everything, he would, she assured herself.

Sometimes he had to go away "on business," but she never pressed him for details on that, either, and he didn't volunteer any. She was unaware that during their courtship, Dix-Mart executive C. W. Strong was as productive as ever, locating a site for yet another Discount City in a small Georgia town that would soon be building a new federal prison, thereby making it a town with steady employment and a strong local economy, ideal conditions for a profitable store.

She knew nothing of the daily calls he made to his office or his senior staff meetings in Mobile or his visits to various Dix-Mart stores, where he followed the company policy of walking the aisles and talking to the sales staff and customers. During the weekday hours each pursued their own course, his Dix-Mart, and hers sophomore English classes at Whitneyville High School.

One day, while Cheyenne appeared to be listening to her students recite the classic "Friends, Romans, Countrymen" passage they'd been assigned to memorize, her mind was lingering on her time with Caleb. There was dinner and evenings at home with the children, long talks and late-night loving that kept getting better, deeper, truly bonding. She'd never known it could be like this, that she could feel this way with any man. Or about any man.

She knew there was talk in the town about her, but she ignored it to the best of her ability. While rumors swirled around her head, as conversations instantly ceased when she appeared on any scene, she simply pretended to be oblivious to it all. She would deliberately fail to respond to any probing, no matter how blatant. Invariably, manners would decree that some other topic of general interest be introduced, but she wondered how long it would take her to become inured to the speculative, sidelong stares that were continually directed toward her.

Had the infamous Penny Sherwood felt this way when she walked the halls of Whitneyville High amidst the whispers and stares of the curious and the proper, upright students?

Cheyenne hadn't seen much of Tricia since the Harpers' fateful dinner party, at which Ben Maitland had indeed broadcast the presence of Caleb Strong in her home. Word had it that the guests had added their own speculations about his presence in her bed as well, and that Tricia was furious with her—though whether for leaving the party early or for sleeping with Caleb Strong, Cheyenne had been unable to ascertain.

"Cheyenne," Tricia had archly informed her, following a two-week silence after the party, "this tawdry affair of yours with Caleb Strong is wrecking your life. There hasn't been this much gossip about anybody in Whitneyville since those trashy Webster twins both got themselves pregnant by that clerk at the hardware store."

Though it was humbling to be categorized with the notorious Webster twins, Cheyenne had replied bravely, "There is nothing tawdry about my love for Caleb."

Tricia was unmoved. "Love? Is that what you're calling it? You've been brainwashed by sex, Cheyenne. Sex, that's all it is. You're a vulnerable widow, and he's taking advantage of you. Give him up before you irreparably damage your reputation."

Cheyenne compared her prior life, with her sterling reputation intact, to her current life, with Caleb Strong in it. One was lonely, sterile and cold; the other exciting and passionate, each day and night richly meaningful. "I won't give him up," she said fiercely.

"He's going to dump you," Tricia said, her tone dire. "He's only using you, Cheyenne. It'll never last, it can't, not between a man like him and a woman like you. Good sex just isn't enough to make a relationship last."

"There's more to our relationship than sex!" Cheyenne cried. She loved so many things about Caleb. His kindness and patience with her children, his generosity and sense of humor. His loyalty to his family. She loved *him*. How she wished she could tell Tricia that Caleb had professed his love for her, that he had mentioned a future together. But she couldn't, of course. Because he hadn't. "There's much, much more, Tricia," she insisted doggedly.

"On your part, maybe. Not his. He'll walk away from you with a shrug, but you're going to be badly hurt, Cheyenne. Don't say I didn't warn you."

Tricia's words had chilled her, but she didn't tell Caleb about the conversation. Nor did she mention that she was being blacklisted from Whitneyville's inner circles. There were parties that she wasn't invited to, meetings and luncheons and get-togethers that were not mentioned to her until after the fact.

Most of the time, she was too filled with contentment and happiness to care. Her life was full and rich with her family and her lover and her job. There were only occasional dark moments alone, when she grappled with anxiety and uncertainty. Caleb still hadn't told her that he loved her or alluded to any permanency in their relationship. She told herself that it didn't matter, that what she had was enough for her. There were times when she actually believed it.

Eleven

Halloween was fast approaching. Caleb bought five pumpkins of varying sizes and carved them into jack-o'-lanterns under Brittany and Jeffrey's directions and advice. The quintet were sitting on the front porch, grinning ghoulishly, when Cheyenne returned home from school one rainy afternoon in late October.

The phone rang as soon as she stepped in the door, and she answered it, expecting to hear Caleb's deep voice over the line. He always called her around this time of day, to make plans for later or, if he was out of town, just to talk. Instead, she heard the cool, well-modulated tones of Janelle Merrit, the wife of Evan's brother, Hunter. Cheyenne grimaced. The Merrits had little to do with her and the children. An obligatory visit Christmas Day with the senior Merrits present was the extent of their family socializing.

Cheyenne knew why they were cold to her. Hunter blamed her for Evan's death. He'd known all about his brother's affair and had told her that if she had been "a better wife," Evan would have been at home instead of in Atlanta the night of his fatal accident.

But what she could never understand was Hunter Merrit's complete indifference to his only brother's two children. She had been alternately angered and saddened by it. Now she simply didn't care. Brittany and Jeffrey had a man in their life whom they played with and looked up to and loved. Caleb Strong.

"Tawny Wheeler asked me to explain," Janelle said in her finishing-school purr, "why she didn't invite Brittany and Jeffrey to her little Amy's Halloween birthday party."

It took a moment for Cheyenne to put the pieces together. Amy Wheeler always celebrated her birthday with a costume party that Brittany and Jeffrey had been attending since they'd all been infants. Cheyenne glanced at the calendar. She hadn't given Amy or her birthday party a single thought until that moment.

"The party was last Sunday afternoon," Janelle continued, "and when I went to the Wheelers' to pick up my little Clifton, I was shocked that Brittany and Jeffrey weren't there. Naturally, I asked Tawny why, thinking perhaps they were ill. That wasn't the case, of course. Tawny felt odd about excluding them, but she thought that since they've been spending so much time with the Strong children—"

"—that they were contaminated or something?" Cheyenne cut in caustically. "The Strongs aren't radioactive, Janelle." Her stomach was churning. Brittany and Jeffrey had been blackballed from a kiddie party because she was dating Caleb Strong!

"Tawny thought that Brittany and Jeffrey might prefer to be with their *new friends* rather than with *our* children," Janelle replied tightly.

As an excuse, it was lame. As a snub, it was quite effective indeed. Cheyenne felt it to the marrow of her bones. But if Janelle expected a gossip-worthy response from her, she was going to be sorely disappointed. Pride kept Cheyenne's voice smooth and steady.

"It was thoughtful of you to call and ask about the children, Janelle. They're both doing quite well and are busy and happy. As am I. Give my love to Hunter and the boys." She hung up before her former sister-in-law could get in another word.

She told Caleb about the call later that evening, after he'd helped her tuck Jeffrey and Brittany into bed. She simply couldn't keep it to herself, not when her children were involved.

"What kind of adult would deliberately want to hurt children by not inviting them to a birthday party?" she raged. "It's incomprehensible to me, Caleb. I've known Tawny Wheeler since our high school days on the cheerleading squad together. I thought I knew her well—until this."

"Brittany and Jeffrey didn't even know about the party," Caleb pointed out. "They aren't hurt. But you are, aren't you, Cheyenne?"

"No! I'm angry and—and baffled."

"Since you've successfully ignored the gossip, rumors, snubs, and disapproval for the past several weeks . . ."

"You know about that?" She stared at him. "You've heard?"

He shrugged. "Of course. And since you seem to be thriving in spite of all the negative talk and sanctions against you, stronger measures must be taken."

"Such as snubbing Brittany and Jeffrey and making sure I realize what's going on." She heaved a troubled sigh. "But why? I really don't understand the maliciousness."

"You're bucking convention, Cheyenne, you're breaking the town's rules. A lady can't get sexually involved with a Strong and still expect to be considered a lady." His expression was hard. "So it follows that you must be punished. And following the principles of guilt-by-association, your children must be punished too."

"Oh," she said softly.

"It's going to get worse, baby." His mouth tightened, his voice grew cool. "Are you having second thoughts? Regrets? Surely you didn't believe that even Cheyenne Whitney could sleep with a Strong without fatal social repercussions?"

She looked straight at him. "I'm not simply sexually involved with you. I'm in love with you, Caleb. And I don't have a single regret."

The passion that tore through him was as urgent and overwhelming as the surge of affection he felt for her. He opened his arms to her, and she walked into them. Stretching up, she kissed his mouth lingeringly, snuggling against him.

"You're as sweet and innocent as a baby, and you're in way too deep," he muttered, rubbing his cheek against her silky hair. She was risking everything— her reputation, her social position, even her children's inherited standing in the town—in this affair with him. His conscience nagged him. They'd both been living in a fool's paradise to think that she could remain unaffected by the gossip and resulting ostracism.

Whitneyville. Once again, the *Town Without Pity* and its narrow-minded inhabitants were shaping the direction of his life . . . and forcing him to leave before he was ready?

Frowning, he held her tighter. "Cheyenne, what am I going to do with you?"

She pretended to consider the question seriously. "Well, the kids are asleep, and Joni Lynn won't be home till ten. That gives us over two hours alone together. You could take me to bed."

Before she'd finished talking, he'd scooped her up in his arms and was striding toward her bedroom. The door was discreetly closed and locked behind them. Burning with sensual intensity, they clung together, glorying in the swift, hot rise of passion.

"I love you," Cheyenne said again and again, as he plunged deeply into her. He took her mouth, silencing her as they rose together in a crescendo of pleasure.

She was almost asleep when she felt Caleb withdraw from her and get out of bed. Her digital alarm clock read 1:46. Raindrops pelted the windowpane. The room was as chilly and dark as the moonless night. Silently, she watched him dress.

"Caleb?" She sat up in bed and flicked on her bedside lamp, just as he headed toward the door.

He turned around. "I thought you were sleeping. Sorry if I woke you, baby." He strode back to her and leaned down, kissing her lightly on her forehead. "Good night, sweetheart."

She reached up and clasped her arms around his neck. "Caleb, I don't want you to go. It's raining. You'll get all wet riding your motorcycle back to the motel."

"I don't melt in water, Cheyenne." He smiled. "That's the unfortunate affliction of the Wicked Witch of the West, not me."

Normally, she would've chuckled at his joke and teased him back. Tonight, she felt too vulnerable and too tightly wired to indulge in humor. "I hate having to leave each other in the middle of the night," she cried, pulling him closer. "Stay with me, Caleb."

He gently pried her hands loose and stepped away from her. "You told me that you didn't want to have to explain my presence in your bed to the children. We both agreed to behave discreetly for their sakes, Cheyenne."

"Caleb, it's almost the end of October. We've been together nearly seven weeks. That's almost two months."

"I'm aware of that, Cheyenne." He regarded her steadily, his tone, his expression, giving nothing away.

Giving nothing . . . She swallowed hard. "You've never once told me that you love me." Her heart was pounding, her eyes feverishly bright. "Do you love me, Caleb?"

It was humiliating to have to ask. What was even worse was watching him withdraw into himself. "I don't like being pressured, Cheyenne," he said tautly.

"You can't accuse me of that! I never ask questions, I never demand answers." Now that she'd started, she couldn't seem to stop. "You know everything there is to know about me, but what I know about you is strictly classified by your own veil of secrecy. I've never complained—"

"Honey, that's exactly what you're doing now. Complaining. You're feeling insecure because your kids weren't invited to an exclusive Whitneyville kiddie gala, and you want some kind of insurance from me that your grand sacrifice is worth it. Well, you'll have to decide that for yourself, Cheyenne."

He turned and walked out the door.

If she weren't naked beneath the sheets, she would have sprung out of bed and followed him. But she was, and she did not possess the temerity to march after him nude. "Come back here, Caleb Strong!" she ordered in a whisper. She didn't dare raise her voice and risk waking the children. "You can't just walk out in the middle of a quarrel. If you leave now, I'll—"

He reappeared in the doorway. "We're not quarreling, Cheyenne. And don't make threats you don't mean and can't carry out." He jauntily blew her a kiss. "Good night, sweetie."

She heard his footsteps along the hall and descending the stairs, heard the front door open and close. She crossed her arms, scowling. Caleb was obviously not taking this quarrel—and that's definitely what it was!—very seriously.

She didn't know whether to be relieved or angry. She ended up feeling depressed. Maybe he didn't take it seriously because he didn't take her seriously. After all, he was so very, very sure of her. She'd given him every reason to be. And she wasn't at all sure of him. Until this moment, that one-sided aspect of their relationship hadn't bothered her. Well, not *too* much. She'd prided herself on not holding back with her own words and feelings, and for not demanding his in reciprocity.

You've never told me you love me. Do you love me? Her plaintive question echoed in her ears, mocking her. She cringed. She wasn't proud of herself tonight. He'd accused her of complaining. From his point of view, perhaps she had been. And not only had he evaded her question, he had walked out, leaving her upset and angry and extremely anxious.

He'll walk away from you with a shrug. This time it was Tricia's voice sounding in her head. Cheyenne pictured Caleb's exit from her room. He hadn't shrugged, had he?

She lay awake for a long, long time, replaying the scene in her mind, examining the slightest nuances, real or imagined. How should she act when she saw him the next day? Angry? Hurt? Or perhaps she should simply pretend that the night's episode hadn't occurred, ignore her lapse and resume her previously successful no-demands policy.

By the time she finally calmed down enough to go back to sleep, the first rays of dawn were streaking the sky. Her alarm went off an hour later. Groggy and groaning, she stumbled out of bed to begin the new day.

Cheyenne glanced at her watch. Four-thirty. Exactly three minutes had passed since she'd last checked the time and still the phone hadn't rung. She'd been trapped in this cycle, checking the time and waiting for the phone to ring, since arriving home from school over an hour ago.

She gazed out the kitchen window to the backyard where Brittany and Jeffrey were running around with Peppy in a boisterous game of their own invention. Joni Lynn wasn't home yet. Cheyenne vaguely remembered her mentioning a yearbook meeting after school.

Why hadn't Caleb called? Their routine hadn't varied in nearly seven weeks. He would call her after school and she would invite him to dinner if he wasn't out of town. While she cooked most of the time, sometimes he took them all out to eat. And they always spent their evenings together, evenings that invariably lasted into the small hours of the morning.

Cheyenne restrained herself from checking her watch again. He wasn't going to call! The realization struck her like a physical blow. Last night . . . Vivid memories kept flashing through her mind. *"Do you love me?"* she had asked. *"I don't like being pressured,"* he had said.

How much did he hate being pressured? she wondered fearfully. Enough to end their relationship? A cold wave of panic swept through her. When he'd left her last night, had it been for the last time?

A cooler, saner, more rational part of her tried to dispel the icy dread that seized her, but it was like trying to hold back a tidal wave with a cardboard screen. The power and force of her fear simply overwhelmed her meager attempts at self-reassurance. After all, her own husband had tired of her, had found her lacking. It was clearly within the realm of possibility that another man might reach the same conclusion about her.

When she heard the doorbell ring, she fairly flew to the front door, praying it was Caleb. It simply had to be! A joyful and relieved smile lit her face. She never should have doubted him. She flung open the door, ready to hurl herself into her lover's arms.

Instead, she received a nasty shock. It was Graham Maitland, not Caleb, who stood on her porch. Her face fell. "Oh," was all she could manage to say. Caleb wasn't here, after all. The worries that she'd light-heartedly banished just seconds ago returned in full measure. It took tremendous effort not to dissolve into tears of bitter disappointment.

"I just wanted to say," Graham began, "that I hope you're satisfied, you traitorous little bitch!"

Cheyenne's jaw dropped. She noticed then that Graham wasn't his usual dapper self. His clothes were disheveled, his hair mussed, and he smelled strongly of alcohol. He was glowering at her, hostility fairly radiating from him. Warily, she took a few steps backward. "I don't understand," she said stiffly.

"You can drop the act!" he snapped. "The game's over. Thanks to your boyfriend, Dix-Mart's payroll and all banking transactions will be handled by the First Dollar Bank in Smithboro. A *Smithboro* bank gets the account, not the *Whitneyville* Bank. And when I accused him, Mr. C. W. Strong, of basing his decision on personal reasons, he had the gall to agree with me! And to laugh about it. He was laughing at me! Strong deliberately chose that nothing of a bank in Smithboro over *our* bank because—"

"Graham, I don't have a clue as to what you're talking about," Cheyenne interrupted. But that fearful, sickening dread was engulfing her once again. Something was very, very wrong, and Caleb—

"You don't have a clue? Oh, that's rich!" Graham said with a snarl. "I suppose you don't know that Caleb Strong, Whitneyville's own loser outcast, is really C. W. Strong, Dix-Mart's future CEO, hand-picked by both Mack Dixon, founder and chairman, and Preston Ralburn, current company president, to succeed them?"

Cheyenne's fingers closed around the top of Great-grandmother Whitney's umbrella stand, and she held on tight. She was too astonished to speak. Things were falling into place with terrifying logic. Caleb Strong, in the guise of Dix-Mart, had been the wolf at Whitneyville's door for four long years. He had finally amassed the power to avenge himself and his family against the town that had shown them no mercy.

Suddenly shivering, she remembered the night he had told her about Graham fathering Joni Lynn. She had looked and listened and thought that Caleb would be an unsparing adversary. Now it appeared that he had taken the most prestigious and financially advantageous account the Whitneyville Bank could ever hope for, let the prospect dazzle the Maitlands for a while, then awarded it to another bank. Unsparing? Oh, yes.

She recalled another chilling memory from that same night. *"The most effective means of revenge is to attack an enemy financially,"* Caleb had said with a matter-of-factness that now struck her as particularly foreboding. He had done exactly that to Whitneyville, by strategically placing a Dix-Mart to drain business from downtown merchants.

". . . or to destroy a carefully built reputation." The second half of his cryptic quote resounded in her head. Whose reputation had he had in mind? *"Surely you didn't believe that even Cheyenne Whitney could sleep with a Strong without fatal social repercussions?"* he had said just the previous night! Suddenly the words took on a sinister meaning, outlining a vengeful goal.

Her doubts and fears must have been reflected in her face and eyes, because Graham's expression grew less enraged. "You didn't know either?" he guessed. "Strong didn't tell you about himself or his plans? Not even today, after the truth about him is all over town?"

She shook her head. "I haven't heard from him today," she whispered. "I've been expecting him to call."

"Strong's left Whitneyville. The Magic Carpet Motel said he checked out. I talked to him there earlier and then tried to reach him again, but he was gone. I had my secretary call"—he paused—"all of the Strongs. They confirmed that he'd left town and wouldn't say where he could be reached or when he'd be back."

Cheyenne felt numb all over, as if she were paralyzed. She could barely even swallow. Caleb had left town without telling her, without calling? She thought of what that implied and felt faint with pain.

Graham stepped inside the vestibule and slumped wearily against the wall. "I'm sorry for what I called you earlier," he mumbled. "It seems you're as much his victim as the bank is. As the whole damn town is!"

"How did you find out about him?" Her face was pale and still.

"We heard through the grapevine that today Dix-Mart requested First Dollar Bank in Smithboro to handle the payroll and all local transactions when the new store opens in the spring. I couldn't believe it. We'd been waiting to get the call from Dix-Mart. . . ." His voice trailed off. "Of course, I had no idea who was in charge of awarding the account. I called Dix-Mart headquarters in Mobile and learned that Caleb Strong is their executive vice-president, the golden boy on the rise. I don't know how or why he landed in that position. Nobody in town does."

"Except the Strongs," Cheyenne murmured.

"Damn the Strongs!" He hit the wall with his fist. "Poor white trash. That's all they are and all they'll ever be!"

She shook her head. "You're wrong, Graham. And it's attitudes like yours that are responsible for this whole business. Why should Caleb give Whitneyville Bank Dix-Mart's account after the way the Maitlands have treated the Strongs, beginning with Crystal and—"

"Don't!" Graham held up his hand, as if to physically ward off her words. "It wasn't my fault! Crystal tried to trap me with that baby. I offered to pay for an abortion, but she wanted to *marry* me! I couldn't do that! A Maitland marry a Strong? Never! I simply refused to cave in to her demands and for revenge, she went through with the pregnancy."

"I don't want to hear your justifications, Graham! The facts are that you seduced Crystal Strong when she was just sixteen years old and you have a child by her, a beautiful, brilliant daughter, and you haven't contributed to her support or shown any interest in her. It's unconscionable. Compound that with the way your family ran Caleb out of town when he was just a boy and I don't blame him for wanting revenge on you any way he could get it."

"Even if you're part of the revenge?" Graham asked cruelly. "You are, you know. How can you stand there and defend him? When Strong decided to screw the town, he obviously decided to do it to one of our women, too, a daughter from one of the first families of Whitneyville." He sneered. "Was it worth it, Cheyenne? Was taking up with a Strong really worth the consequences?"

"You might ask yourself that question, Mr. Maitland." The sound of the clear, young voice caused both Cheyenne and Graham to whirl around. Joni Lynn stood behind them in the hall. How long she'd been there was anybody's guess. Neither had heard her come into the house.

Joni Lynn's dark eyes, so like her father's in color and shape, were glittering with emotion. "Cheyenne isn't the only one who took up with a Strong. You did too, Mr. Maitland," she said coldly. "You and my mother. Was it worth the consequences for you? Losing the Dix-Mart account for your bank? Having a daughter you've never acknowledged?"

"Oh, Joni Lynn," Cheyenne breathed. "You—You heard."

"Everything." Joni Lynn stared at Graham. "So you're my father. All my life I've wondered who he was and for the past year I've been living just two blocks away from him."

Graham ran his hand through his hair. "I can't deal with this now," he exclaimed, wild-eyed. He fled from the house without a backward glance.

"Joni Lynn." Cheyenne moved toward the girl.

"Honey, I'm so sorry that you had to find out this way."

"No big deal." Joni Lynn shrugged in a way so reminiscent of Caleb, Cheyenne's heart ached. "Look at it this way, Cheyenne. At least I know my father is a big-shot bank president from a respectable family, instead of a serial killer on death row somewhere. Excuse me, I have to make a phone call." She started down the hall.

Cheyenne followed her. "Joni Lynn, I know how much this must hurt—"

"Police? This is Joni Lynn Strong. I want to report a drunk driver."

Cheyenne gasped as she heard Joni Lynn give a description of Graham Maitland's car and license number to the police. "They said they'll pick him up," she said after hanging up.

"Joni Lynn . . ."

"There was a time when the Whitneyville police were run by people like the Maitlands and the Thurmans, but not anymore," Joni Lynn said, fending off the arm that Cheyenne attempted to put around her shoulders. "After our cousin Rusty was falsely arrested and beaten up last spring, Uncle Caleb reported the police department to the state attorney general and the justice department for violating Rusty's civil rights. They've been under investigation ever since—and now they're very careful to follow proper procedure." She smiled slightly. "And they're quite responsive to the name Strong. Uncle Caleb says we have nothing to fear from them anymore."

"The Strongs have nothing to fear from anybody anymore," Cheyenne said softly. "Your uncle Caleb has finally seen to that."

"Cheyenne, I'm going to spend the night at home with my mother," Joni Lynn said. In spite of her insouciant air, her young face was shadowed with sadness and disillusionment. "She and I have a lot to talk about."

"I know," Cheyenne said softly. "But first, will you tell me about Caleb and Dix-Mart?"

Joni Lynn nodded, brightening. "I'm glad I can tell you at last. It's one of my favorite stories. Uncle Caleb met Karen Dixon Ralburn, Mr. Mack Dixon's only child and Preston Ralburn's wife, about six months after he left Whitneyville." Her smile twisted into a bitter grimace. "That is, after *my father* and the other Maitlands ran him out of town."

"Please go on, Joni Lynn," Cheyenne said, fighting the stinging pain that assailed her. She deeply regretted that the girl had learned the truth about her father in such a heartbreakingly cold way.

"Uncle Caleb was on his motorcycle on a highway near Mobile, and he saw this woman lose control of her car when the tire blew out. The car went over an embankment and flipped. Uncle Caleb went down to help. He was the only one to stop," Joni Lynn added, her eyes shining with pride. "Everybody else just drove past, but he got Karen and her two little girls out of the car, carried them up the hill, and flagged down a car to summon help."

Cheyenne pictured the Caleb she had known all those years ago, a teenage rebel on his own, banished from his home. Yet he had stopped to help a woman and children in distress. "Oh, Caleb," she whispered. Her eyes filled with tears.

"Mr. Dixon and his son-in-law were so grateful to Uncle Caleb for stopping to help Karen and the little girls that they offered him anything he wanted," Joni Lynn continued. "A big cash reward, a new car, anything. But Uncle Caleb said what he wanted most was a steady job and a room to live in. He'd been traveling around the country on his own, doing odd jobs along the way and sort of crashing wherever he could. He was sick of it. He said he'd finally grown up and realized that he didn't want to live that way anymore. Uncle Caleb still didn't know who the Dixons were or their connection to Dix-Mart. He didn't learn until after they got him a job as a stock boy in the Mobile Dix-Mart."

"And he worked his way from a stock boy without a high school diploma to future president of the company?" Cheyenne asked, awed.

Joni Lynn nodded. "He got himself a room in Mobile and worked at Dix-Mart, and one day he noticed that the stockroom manager was stealing the merchandise and then selling it on the black market for his own profit. He offered to pay Uncle Caleb a cut to keep quiet about it." Her voice rose dramatically. "Do you know what Uncle Caleb did? He went right to Dix-Mart headquarters and asked to see Mack Dixon. He said he was tired of everybody expecting the Strongs to be corruptible and that he'd never rip off the Dixons, not when they'd given him this job and this chance. So he reported the embezzler, and old Mr. Mack was so impressed with his honesty, he decided Caleb Strong had a big future with Dix-Mart. He told Uncle Caleb to get his high school equivalency GED and the company would pay for him to go to college. And that's what happened. Uncle Caleb got a degree in business from Auburn University and later his MBA from Duke. He's worked for Dix-Mart ever since."

It was an inspiring rags-to-riches tale, but one with a dark edge, Cheyenne thought bleakly. Caleb had never forgotten the town and the people who had wronged him and his family. There had been a score to settle, and he'd done that. Unfortunately, it seemed she'd been part of that score.

Though Cheyenne tried to talk her in to staying, Joni Lynn was adamant about facing her mother with her newfound information. Cheyenne cried after she left. The tears she'd been holding at bay all day couldn't be suppressed any longer. Feelings of grief and loss and betrayal churned within her, so intermingled that she couldn't begin to separate them.

Too much had changed in the past twenty-four hours, all the results of Caleb's actions. He had deliberately chosen to reveal himself at last, and Cheyenne traced the timing of his decision to their unhappy little scene in her bedroom. It was obvious he was tired of her. Her demand for a declaration of love from him had sealed her fate. He'd ended the game by playing his trump card, calling the banks. Then he had left town. His revenge was over. And that meant the end of her too.

But even knowing that, even as his motives for making her fall in love with him became heartbreakingly clear, Cheyenne found herself wishing she hadn't uttered that plea for love. If she hadn't, he might have stayed awhile longer. He might be there with her right now, prolonging his revenge before thrusting the final parry.

And even though she now knew how it would end, she still wanted him more than she'd ever wanted anything or anyone in her entire life.

Twelve

Two of the longest and loneliest days of Cheyenne's life passed at an interminably slow pace. To her students and fellow teachers, she appeared to be her same, serene self. Nobody guessed that inside she was shattered and silently screaming with pain. She was an excellent actress, Cheyenne guessed, undoubtedly from all those years of pretending to be alive when she'd been dead inside. The intensity of the pain she was feeling now made her almost nostalgic for those days when she'd been numb and frozen.

Her business-as-usual facade didn't work as well on the home front. She found herself thinking too much and on the verge of tears too often. Joni Lynn had decided to stay with her mother awhile longer as they unraveled the grim details of their past. Brittany and Jeffrey couldn't understand both Joni Lynn's and "Uncle Caleb's" absence and asked for and about them constantly. Cheyenne found herself doing anything to distract them, including letting them watch television for too many hours, giving them junk food on demand, even skipping bedtime until they fell asleep on the sofa in front of the TV.

As she wandered into the living room that second

night and saw the children sleeping there, still dressed in their school clothes, the remains of a cookies-popcorn-and-soda feast strewn around the room, and the TV flickering, she was assailed by a terrible case of maternal guilt. This was no way to raise children! She had to pull herself together.

While she was berating herself, Peppy suddenly sat up and cocked his ears. Cheyenne groaned. Probably the last thing she felt like doing right now was taking the dog out. "Go back to sleep, boy," she implored. "I'll let you out later, I promise."

But Peppy was already on his feet. Barking, he bounded to the door. Cheyenne could hear him running around in circles in the front hall, yipping. That wasn't his take-me-out behavior, it was his there's-someone-coming routine. She hadn't heard anything, but then, who could with the television so loud? She turned down the volume before joining Peppy in the vestibule. Peering through the small window in the front door, she saw Peppy was right. A sports car had just pulled up in front of the house.

Cheyenne froze. She didn't recognize the car and couldn't fathom who might be coming to visit at ten o'clock at night. Surely not Ben Maitland . . . She'd received a verbally abusive call from Ben shortly after his brother Graham had been arrested by the Whitneyville police for driving while intoxicated. The Maitland brothers believed she was the one who'd called the police, and she hadn't disabused them of the notion. Relations were strained enough between the Maitlands and the Strongs without adding an arrest to the score.

She'd received other calls, too, these past two days, none of them heartening. From Tricia, Hunter Merrit, and Dawn Bentley, among others. Nobody but Graham believed she hadn't been in on Caleb Strong's secret from the start. Nobody knew Caleb had left her, either, and even if they had, Cheyenne knew she wouldn't have received an iota of sympathy.

In the course of forty-eight hours, she'd become Whitneyville's own Benedict Arnold. Socially, she knew she was well and truly finished in the town.

And she didn't care. She doubted she ever would. For the first time in her life, the world beyond Whitneyville beckoned. She'd loved Atlanta when she'd gone there with Caleb. If she moved there, she and the children could begin a whole new life. . . .

Peppy was going wild now, jumping up and down and barking excitedly. Cheyenne heard footsteps on the porch and opened the door before the doorbell could be rung. If she was about to be excoriated again by another outraged former friend, she didn't want Brittany and Jeffrey awakened for it.

Caleb Strong stood on the porch. Smiling.

It was the smile that did it. Cheyenne felt rage burn through her, as swift and searing as a forest fire in a drought. He had the gall to come back here and gloat? She slammed the door shut.

"Cheyenne?" he called, and began to rap on the door.

She stormed down the hall, out of earshot, leaving Peppy to paw at the door and whimper worriedly. She strode into the kitchen, her legs shaking so much, she had difficulty walking straight. Moments later, Peppy joined her and lunged at the kitchen door, telling her Caleb was about to appear there.

He did, knocking and calling her name. "Go away!" she ordered.

There was a momentary silence, and she thought he had obeyed her. She collapsed onto a chair, about to break into tears when the sound of his voice brought her to her feet once again. "Dammit, Cheyenne, if you don't open the damn door this instant, I'm going to break it down."

Galvanized, she flung open the door. "Stop swearing! I told you to go away and I meant it!" She tried to slam the door shut, but this time he was prepared and caught it with both hands. Giving a push, he shoved his way inside.

"What's going on, Cheyenne?" He was no longer smiling, and his voice was rough. He looked as outraged as she felt.

"You can even ask me that? How stupid do you think I am, Caleb?" She was insulted. "Did you really think I'd welcome you with open arms after what you did?"

"Yeah, I did think that." His eyes suddenly were as cold as blue ice.

His frankness took her aback. "I can understand that, I suppose," she said bitterly. "I'd given you every reason to believe—"

"—that you loved me. That you valued me over this damn town."

"But that didn't matter to you, Caleb. *I* didn't matter to you. You used me for revenge and when you were through, you dumped me and—"

"Do you mind telling me what the hell you're talking about?" he snapped.

Cheyenne gulped. He seemed to tower over her, big and threatening and so terribly angry. She took a step backward. Where had she heard that the best defense was an offensive strike? Facing him now, she figured it was worth a try. "I asked you to stop cursing," she said with far less vehemence than the directive required.

"Then stop giving me reasons to curse. And explain this I-used-you-for-revenge-and-then-dumped-you crap."

"You did!" she cried, her voice breaking.

Quick as a flash, his hand snaked out to catch her wrist, and he yanked her toward him. "The hell I did!" Another swift tug brought her tumbling against him. His arms encircled her, and he gazed down at her, his eyes glittering. "Why would I, when I'm crazy about you? I love you, you little idiot." He gave her a small shake, then hugged her close. "I love you."

Not quite a romantic hearts-and-flowers declaration, but it affected Cheyenne as if it were. Her eyes filled with emotional tears, and her whole body flushed with a warming, healing glow of happiness. "Oh, Caleb!" She gazed up at him, her heart in her eyes. "I—I thought that you . . ."

"You already told me what you thought," he said raspily, "and it's the stupidest thing I've ever heard. How could you believe such a thing? How could you doubt me that way, Cheyenne? I don't understand. I've been away from Whitneyville for less than forty-eight hours, and in that short time you managed to dream up some wild paranoid tale of—"

"You haven't called me," she wailed. "Not once in two whole days! We quarreled that night, and I haven't heard from you since. Graham told me about Dix-Mart, and then you left town and—" She pulled back a little, stiffening. "What was I supposed to think? You never told me you loved me until this minute. You said you didn't want to be pressured and—"

"Relax," he said softly, drawing her closer again. His big hands moved over her caressively. "I concede that I mishandled the situation that night, but I didn't consider it a quarrel, Cheyenne. I told you that then. I did realize that it was time to make my move, and to be honest, I was reluctant to do so. I discovered that I loved having you love me as Caleb Strong, town misfit. I liked the way things were developing between us. I was enjoying being with you and the children. I admit I wasn't in any hurry to move on to the next stage. Call it a bachelor's instinct to preserve the status quo, if you will. But your ultimatum that night—"

"I didn't mean it as an ultimatum, I just wanted—"

"—me to tell you I love you," he said, smiling now. All his angry tension seemed to drain away. "And for me to ask you to marry me," he added humorously. "I wasn't ready that night. I wanted to come clean with the town first. Now your wish is about to be granted, sweetheart. I love you and want to marry you. I want to adopt your kids and raise them as my own, and I want you to have my baby. Babies," he amended. "At least two more would be nice. We'll live in Mobile, of course. We can start looking for a bigger house right away."

She gaped at him. "I don't know what to say. I thought it was over."

"It's not over, Cheyenne. It'll never be over. Now, say yes. This is my first proposal ever, and I want a positive answer."

"Yes!" She blinked back the tears that pooled in her eyes. "Oh, Caleb, yes! I love you so much. When I thought you were gone, I—" She broke off.

She didn't want to dwell on how miserable she'd been. Caleb was here and he loved her, and she couldn't wait to begin living happily ever after with him. But there were a few things she needed to get straight, a few questions that definitely needed answers. Such as: "Why did you leave town without telling me, Caleb? And why haven't you called me for the past two days?"

"Honey, I tried to call."

She arched her brows skeptically.

"Hmm, maybe I'd better take this from the top." He sat down on a chair, pulling her onto his lap. "After I blew my cover, you know, gave Dix-Mart's business to the Smithboro bank and revealed my position with the company to the Maitlands, I received a call from headquarters. There'd been a gas line explosion in one of our northern Arkansas stores. I flew out there immediately. It was a crisis situation, and I had to be there. The entire executive staff went directly to the scene."

His expression sobered. "One person was killed, three were seriously injured, and about a dozen more were treated at the local hospital for minor injuries. Since then, I've been so busy, I've barely had time to sleep or eat. I've been swamped making phone calls, visiting the families, meeting with gas company officials and lawyers."

He touched her face, and his voice deepened. "One of the phone calls I tried to make was to you. I must have called a dozen times. Every time I tried, I either got a busy signal or no one was home."

"I have been on the phone a lot," she admitted sheepishly, remembering all those outraged calls she'd received. "And I unplugged the phone both last night and tonight."

He shrugged. "It was frustrating not being able to reach you, but I didn't worry about it. I was only gone two days. It never entered my head that you'd think I had deliberately abandoned you as part of some crazy revenge plot."

Now that she was in full possession of the facts, now that she was sitting there warm and safe in his arms, the whole notion did seem incredibly stupid. She had shown an appalling lack of faith and trust in him, she reprimanded herself. "I'm sorry, Caleb," she said softly. "For not believing what I should have believed, based on these past seven weeks with you."

He smiled and tightened his arms around her. "Let's call it a draw, baby. I shouldn't have sauntered out of your bedroom that night without telling you what you deserved to know—how much you and Brittany and Jeffrey mean to me, that I love you and want all of you permanently in my life."

He stood up, still holding her in his arms, and carried her from the kitchen. They passed the living room, where Brittany and Jeffrey were sound asleep on the sofa. Caleb quirked a questioning eyebrow.

"Let's put them in their own beds later," Cheyenne whispered. "Right now I need to be alone with you. In my room. In my bed."

Caleb grinned sexily as he started up the stairs. "The lady's wish is my command."

THE EDITOR'S CORNER

As summer draws to a close, the nights get colder, and what better way could there be to warm up than by reading these fabulous LOVESWEPTs we have in store for you next month.

Joan Elliott Pickart leads the list with THE DEVIL IN STONE, LOVESWEPT #492, a powerful story of a love that flourishes despite difficult circumstances. When Robert Stone charges into Winter Holt's craft shop, he's a warrior on the warpath, out to expose a con artist. But he quickly realizes Winter is as honest as the day is long, and as beautiful as the desert sunrise. He longs to kiss away the sadness in her eyes, but she's vowed never to give her heart to another man—especially one who runs his life by a schedule and believes that love can be planned. It takes a lot of thrilling persuasion before Robert can convince Winter that their very different lives can be bridged. This is a romance to be cherished.

Humorous and emotional, playful and poignant, HEART OF DIXIE, LOVESWEPT #493, is another winner from Tami Hoag. Who can resist Jake Gannon, with his well-muscled body and blue eyes a girl can drown in? Dixie La Fontaine sure tries as she tows his overheated car to Mare's Nest, South Carolina. A perfect man like him would want a perfect woman, and that certainly isn't Dixie. But Jake knows a special lady when he sees one, and he's in hot pursuit of her down-home charm and all-delicious curves. If only he can share the secret of why he came to her town in the first place . . . A little mystery, a touch of Southern magic, and a lot of white-hot passion—who could ask for anything more?

A handsome devil of a rancher will send you swooning in THE LADY AND THE COWBOY, LOVESWEPT #494, by Charlotte Hughes. Dillon McKenzie is rugged, rowdy, and none too pleased that Abel Pratt's will divided his ranch equally between Dillon and a lady preacher! He doesn't want any goody-two-shoes telling him what to do, even one whose skin is silk and whose eyes light up the dark places in his heart. Rachael Caitland is determined to make the best of things, but the rough-and-tumble cowboy makes her yearn to risk caring for a man who's all wrong for her. Once Dillon tastes Rachael's fire, he'll move heaven and earth to make her break her rules. Give yourself a treat, and don't miss this compelling romance.

In SCANDALOUS, LOVESWEPT #495, Patricia Burroughs creates an unforgettable couple in the delectably brazen Paisley Vandermeir and the very respectable but oh so sexy Christopher Quincy Maitland. Born to a family constantly in the scandal sheets, Paisley is determined to commit one indiscretion and retire from notoriety. But when she throws herself at Chris, who belongs to another, she's shocked to find him a willing partner. Chris has a wild streak that's subdued by a comfortable engagement, but the intoxicating Paisley tempts him to break free. To claim her for his own, he'll brave trouble and reap its sweet reward. An utterly delightful book that will leave you smiling and looking for the next Patricia Burroughs LOVESWEPT.

Olivia Rupprecht pulls out all the stops in her next book, BEHIND CLOSED DOORS, LOVESWEPT #496, a potent love story that throbs with long-denied desire. When widower Myles Wellington learns that his sister-in-law, Faith, is carrying his child, he insists that she move into his house. Because she's loved him for so long and has been so alone, Faith has secretly agreed to help her sister with the gift of a child to Myles. How can she live with the one man who's forbidden to her, yet how can she resist grabbing at the chance to be with the only man whose touch sets her soul on fire? Myles wants this child, but he soon discovers he wants Faith even more. Together they struggle to break free of the past and exult in a passionate union. . . . Another fiery romance from Olivia.

Suzanne Forster concludes the month with a tale of smoldering sensuality, PRIVATE DANCER, LOVESWEPT #497. Sam Nichols is a tornado of sexual virility, and Bev Brewster has plenty of reservations about joining forces with him to hunt a con man on a cruise ship. Still, the job must be done, and Bev is professional enough to keep her distance from the deliciously dangerous Sam. But close quarters and steamy nights spark an inferno of ecstasy. Before long Sam's set her aflame with tantalizing caresses and thrilling kisses. But his dark anguish shadows the fierce pleasure they share. Once the chase is over and the criminal caught, will Sam's secret pain drive them apart forever?

Do remember to look for our FANFARE novels next month—four provocative and memorable stories with vastly different settings and times. First is GENUINE LIES by bestselling author Nora Roberts, a dazzling novel of Hollywood glamour, seductive secrets, and truth that can kill. MIRACLE by bestselling LOVESWEPT author Deborah Smith is an unforgettable story of love and the collision of worlds, from a shanty in the Georgia hills to a television studio in L.A. With warm, humorous, passionate characters, MIR-ACLE weaves a spell in which love may be improbable but never impossible. Award-winning author Susan Johnson joins the FAN-FARE list with her steamiest historical romance yet, FORBIDDEN. And don't miss bestselling LOVESWEPT author Judy Gill's BAD BILLY CULVER, a fabulous tale of sexual awakening, scandal, lies, and a passion that can't be denied.

We want to wish the best of luck to Carolyn Nichols, Publisher of LOVESWEPT. After nine eminently successful years, Carolyn has decided to leave publishing to embark on a new venture to help create jobs for the homeless. Carolyn joined Bantam Books in the spring of 1982 to create a line of contemporary romances. LOVESWEPT was launched to instant acclaim in May of 1983, and is now beloved by millions of fans worldwide. Numerous authors, now well-known and well-loved by loyal readers, have Carolyn to thank for daring to break the time-honored rules of romance writing, and for helping to usher in a vital new era of women's fiction.

For all of us here at LOVESWEPT, working with Carolyn has been an ever-stimulating experience. She has brought to her job a vitality and creativity that has spread throughout the staff and, we hope, will remain in the years to come. Carolyn is a consummate editor, a selfless, passionate, and unpretentious humanitarian, a loving mother, and our dear, dear friend. Though we will miss her deeply, we applaud her decision to turn her unmatchable drive toward helping those in need. We on the LOVESWEPT staff—Nita Taublib, Publishing Associate; Beth de Guzman, Editor; Susann Brailey, Consulting Editor; Elizabeth Barrett, Consulting Editor; and Tom Kleh, Assistant to the Publisher of Loveswept—vow to continue to bring you the best stories of consistently high quality that make each one a "keeper" in the best LOVESWEPT tradition.

Happy reading!

With every good wish,

Nita Taublib

Nita Taublib
Publishing Associate
LOVESWEPT/FANFARE
Bantam Books
New York, NY 10103

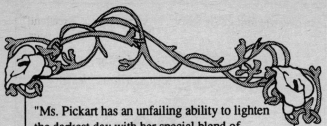

"Ms. Pickart has an unfailing ability to lighten the darkest day with her special blend of humor and romance." *--Romantic Times*

THE BONNIE BLUE

by Joan Elliott Pickart

Slade Ironbow was big, dark, and dangerous, a man any woman would want -- and the one rancher Becca Colten found impossible to resist!

Nobody could tame the rugged half-Apache with the devil's eyes, but when honor and a secret promise brought him to the Bonnie Blue ranch as her new foreman, Becca couldn't send him away. She needed his help to keep from losing her ranch to the man she suspected had murdered her father, but stubborn pride made her fight the mysterious loner whose body left her breathless and whose touch made her burn with needs she'd never understood.

THE SYMBOL OF GREAT WOMEN'S FICTION FROM BANTAM

On sale now at your local bookstore.

FANFARE

Enter the marvelous new world of **Fanfare**!
From sweeping historicals set around the globe to
contemporary novels set in glamorous spots,
Fanfare means great reading.
Be sure to look for new **Fanfare** titles each month!

Coming Soon:

TEXAS! CHASE

By *New York Times* bestselling author, **Sandra Brown**

The reckless rodeo rider who'd lost everything he loved...
Bittersweet, sensual, riveting, TEXAS! CHASE will touch every heart.

THE MATCHMAKER

By **Kay Hooper**, author of STAR-CROSSED LOVERS

Sheer magic in a romance of forbidden love between rich and mysterious
Cyrus Fortune and the exquisite beauty he is bound to rescue.

RAINBOW

By **Patricia Potter**

A flirt without consequence . . . a rogue without morals . . . From a fierce,
stormy passion rose a love as magnificent as a rainbow.

FOLLOW THE SUN

By **Deborah Smith**, author of THE BELOVED WOMAN

Three women bound by the blood of their noble Cherokee ancestors . . .
one glorious legacy of adventure, intrigue -- and passion!